COVER ME UP

BOOK ONE

THE BRIDGESTONES OF MONTANA

JULIANA STONE

Editing by Linda Ingmanson

Cover Design: JS Designs Cover Art

Photo: Wander Aguiar

CHAPTER 1

THE CELL PHONE SHOULD HAVE WOKEN HIM, BUT IT WAS THE loud banging on the door that cut through Cal Bridgestone's whiskey-soaked dreams. With a groan, he swore under his breath and slid one eye open. A mess of blonde hair and the kind of tanned skin only achieved from a spray bottle filled his vision. He blinked again and slowly rolled onto his other side, only to find another warm body splayed across the bed. This one a brunette. Short pixie hair, long muscular legs, and in possession of more tattoos than any man he knew.

A crooked smile slid across his face. She'd been bendy, that one.

The banging got louder, and he frowned, moving the snoring brunette enough for him to slide into a seated position at the end of a bed that could fit five. Easily. Brain a little foggy, he gave his head a shake (wrong thing to do) and swore as pain radiated across his forehead. It took a bit, but his eyes adjusted, and Cal peered through the gloom at the clothes scattered across the floor. A sliver of sunlight had managed to find its way inside from between the heavy blinds that fell across the lavish suite, and he spied a lacy pink bra hanging from the chandelier over the bed. As his eyes sharpened some more and moved across the room, he saw the matching undies among the empty bottles of booze that cluttered the large coffee table, or as his housekeeper Janet called it, an *occasional* table. Champagne glasses, one on its side, were perched on top of the bar along with an empty liquor bottle, and there appeared to be some broken glass on the floor nearby.

"Damn," he muttered. *That was one hell of a night*. His frown deepened as he got to his feet and searched for his boxers. He found them bundled up in the corner where the blonde had pulled them off the night before and, after sliding them on, ran his hands through the tangle of hair at his nape.

He wondered where the boys were, his guitarist Matty and drummer Ollie in particular, because they'd come back after the show. A small groan escaped his lips as another round of pain shot through his head. It could have been because of what undoubtedly was going to be an epic hangover, but he was betting it was on account of a renewed banging at the door.

He was getting too old for this shit.

He swore under his breath as he made his way through the suite and over to the door. "Calm down." He opened it just as Ivy Wilkens, his best friend and PA, was about to kick the damn thing in. "What the hell?"

"I've been calling your cell for two hours." She was pissed and not trying to hide it.

"I don't know where my cell is."

"Shocking." The sarcasm, man, it was heavy.

He had nothing for that. Not that it mattered, because she went on, her voice rising with each word.

"And why are the phones in your suite not working?"

He winked at her because he knew it would piss her off even more. "I had a little party last night and told them I didn't want to be disturbed."

"Them?" she shot back. "Who is them?"

He gave her a moment. She was not happy with him. "The people at the front desk?"

She gave him a look that was part exasperation and part something else. If he was fully awake and in charge of his faculties, he might have been concerned about the something else, but as it was, Cal's frown deepened. It was too early for her to be on fire about something he'd done between the show the night before and right now. Heck, it was just normal shenanigans, as far as he could remember. The boys in the band, a couple of girls, and a whole lot of Mr. Daniels.

"What's going on?" he asked.

She held his gaze for all of two seconds before her eyes slid from his and she moved past him, toward the bed, which was perched on a pedestal at the far end of the suite. Cal grabbed a water bottle from the bar and waited for the shitstorm to hit. The girls would want to stay—they always did—but Ivy wasn't in the mood. That much was clear.

She found the remote for the blinds, and sunlight filled the room as she walked over to the bed, throwing clothes at the girls and telling them to get the hell up as she did so. Neither one of them listened, though the brunette managed a middle-finger salute.

Shit, this was gonna be good.

Ivy found a pinkish sparkly boot and threw it at the bed, missing little pixie cut by an inch and hitting the wall with a thud.

"You bitch!" the woman yelled. "If that hit me, I could have you charged with assault."

She wasn't wrong, but what she didn't know was that back in the day, Ivy was the best damn shortstop the Wolverines had ever seen, and she could have hit her square in the face. If she'd wanted to, that was.

Ivy said nothing. She picked up the second boot, and it landed in the same spot as the first. Almost instantly, there was a shriek that cut through the fog in Cal's head, followed by a string of profanity that would impress most of the men he knew—and they could swear like truckers. He took a swig of water, impressed with pixie cut's vocabulary, and after a bunch more swearing and a whole lot of shouting, she stumbled off the bed, clutching a shimmery blue dress across her breasts. The blonde finally poked up her head and moved her hair from her face, eyes already seductive and on the prowl as they slid from Cal to Ivy.

"What's going on?" she asked, stretching her arms far above her head and putting her silicone-filled double D's on display. "Why do you have to be so loud?"

"I'm guessing you're the pink dress." Ivy tossed a few slips of material onto the bed. "Mr. Bridgestone would like to thank you for accompanying him back from the show, but it's time to go."

"Cal," the blonde said, making one syllable stretch into two. She turned to him, her voice raspy from what he guessed was a pack-a-day habit. An exaggerated pout made her overly plump mouth look ridiculous. "You said we could go to the next show with you."

"That sure would have been fun, but darlin'..." He pointed to the slim redhead whose narrowed eyes were about to spew bullets. "Ivy here says it's time to shut down our little party and, well, she kind of runs things." He kept his tone light, but truthfully in the harsh light of day, he was embarrassed for Ivy to be here with him.

The blonde shot a hateful look at Ivy before turning back to him. "You're Cal Fucking Bridgestone. Who cares what some dumb chick with glasses the size of coke bottles says?"

"Well now," he said as he pulled his jeans off the edge of the sofa. "Why'd you have to go and insult Ivy like that?" He zipped up and nodded to the door, his eyes wintry, his tone sharp. "Like the lady said, it's time to leave."

The girls knew he meant business. "You're an asshole," pixie cut bit out on her way by.

"I've been called worse."

"He sure has," Ivy retorted for good measure. "By me."

He didn't give the blonde a chance to say anything and slammed the door shut behind her, then slowly cracked his neck and stretched.

"You have awful taste in groupies, you know that right?"

Cal ignored Ivy's comment. He'd give his left pinky for a bacon and egg.

"Now, what the hell is so important you had to interrupt round two before it even had a chance to start?" He turned back to her and immediately went still. Ivy's blue eyes, large and magnified by her glasses, were somber as they gazed across the room at him. For the first time, he noticed her rumpled clothes and the fact that she'd pulled on her top so quick, she hadn't taken the time to button it up properly. Her long dark red hair was a tangled mess, secured on top of her head in a loose knot that would fall apart with one tug.

"Ivy?" He took two steps toward her and paused, his gut turning over as her mouth opened and the words spilled from between her lips.

"There's been an accident." Her voice was halting and

low, hitting a timbre that was somewhere between bad news and *really* bad news. "Your brother."

His gut clenched, an involuntary movement that brought with it a roll of nausea and the kind of sweat that covered his body in an instant sheen. He could have blamed it on the tequila or the Jack, but that would have been too easy. This was a visceral reaction because he *knew* what was coming would be about as far from good as you could get.

"How bad?" he asked slowly, his tongue so thick, it was hard to swallow.

"Bad." Ivy was never one to sugarcoat. "Or at least, not great. I don't know many details."

He looked out the window and saw a plane slice through the bright blue sky, a tail of smoke fading in its wake. In the distance, Sydney Harbor glistened like diamonds, and the sight of it reminded Cal that he was as far from Montana as a man could get.

"Who?" he managed to say as he exhaled and glanced Ivy's way. He had two brothers and two sisters. His youngest brother, Ryland, was a senior in high school, and the other...

"Bent."

Benton Bodean Bridgestone. Bent was the oldest and had eight years on Cal. He'd practically raised Cal and the rest of the Bridgestones after their mother died, and as a youngster, Cal had worshipped Bent. They'd been so damn tight, closer than anyone he'd known, but life had a way of making some things that seem certain break apart, and Cal hadn't seen or talked to his brother in nearly six years. Not since that Christmas Eve when punches were thrown on both sides and things were said, the kind of things you don't take back.

The kind of things that cut through flesh and bone to become silent wounds that settle in hearts and souls and never heal. Regret, the kind that chokes a man up and fills his throat with sawdust, made it impossible to speak. Cal could only stare at Ivy wordlessly, waiting for the hammer to fall.

"We need to get you back to the States right away. I've got the jet waiting. Vivian should be there when we arrive, but no one can get hold of Scarlett. She's apparently backpacking somewhere in Europe. I've been in touch with her friends, and I've left messages so as soon as she checks in, which"—Ivy paused her forehead scrunched—"I'm hoping will be by tomorrow latest, we'll get her home. Don't worry about the rest of the tour dates. We've already rescheduled the European leg and the last show here as well. A press release will go out after we've arrived in Montana. I want you to have some time before it all hits. It's good that we had three days between shows, so no one needs to know yet."

"When did this happen?" His voice was so low, he barely heard his own words.

Ivy hesitated, and then whispered, "Three days ago."

Anger flared as his head shot up. "Why the hell am I just finding out now?"

"I don't know," she replied softly. "I don't have any details other than that it's important to get back as soon as we can."

"Because he's not gonna make it."

"That's not what I was told, and that's not what I said. Let's just get home, and then we can see where things are at."

Ivy was right. There was no use speculating when he didn't know jack shit. His vision blurred at the thought of Bent lying in a hospital bed. It twisted him up in a way that should have been surprising considering the state of things, but it wasn't. How many times had he grabbed his cell to call Bent? To tell him his last album had gone triple platinum in a week? That he held the record for the most downloaded songs ever?

Hell, just a month ago, he'd bought a new stallion, a beautiful paint he planned to breed at his new spread in California, and he'd dialed the house before he knew what he was doing. When he heard Bent's voice on the other end, he'd frozen up and all those words tangled inside him like a ball of thread wound so tight, it would never come apart. And like a twelve-year-old idiot, he'd hung up without saying anything.

Him. A grown-ass man of thirty. And now he might not get a chance to speak to his brother again.

He glanced down at his bare feet and spied his boots in the corner, near the bar. He was halfway across the room before he stopped cold and rasped, "What about Daisy Mae?"

"She's still not in the picture," she said slowly. "No one has heard from her in about four years."

He had more questions, but couldn't seem to get them out. What about little Nora?

That regret inside him was starting to get big. So damn big he could barely swallow. He said nothing more and got dressed, and while Ivy gathered the rest of his stuff, his guitar, and some clothes, he emptied the contents of his stomach into the garbage can.

A bodyguard met them outside the suite and helped them carry everything down to the lobby where, even at this time of day, a crowd of fans lay in wait. He ignored them all, which was not the norm, and slipped into a large black SUV that would take him to a private airstrip outside the city. To a jet that would take him back to Montana. Back to the Bridgestone Ranch. To a brother who was broken and maybe dying. To a father he had no relationship with. A family scattered with one sister in Alaska and the other in New York City when she wasn't galivanting around the world. All of them frayed ends of a thread that was blowing in the wind, unspooling faster than they realized.

Cal was headed back to a past he'd been running from all his life, it seemed. A past rich with heartache and enough tragedy to fuel the songs he wrote. Songs that had made him the number-one country star in the world and gave him everything he thought he'd ever wanted.

And yet as he climbed the stairs of the private plane, bought and paid for with his own money, and took a window seat far from Ivy and his publicist and manager, he couldn't help but think that he'd gotten it all wrong. None of this felt right or good or satisfying. Because at the end of the day, he was just a cowboy singing songs into the dark, alone.

Always alone.

He took out his cell and ran his fingers over his contacts, eyes lingering on a name, thinking of a woman who disliked him more than anyone on the planet. A woman who had every right to feel that way.

He should just leave her alone. That would be the right thing to do. Wouldn't it? The plane's engines rumbled beneath him, and before he could talk himself out of it, Cal hit up a number he hadn't called since before he'd left Montana. The fact it was still in his contacts said something. It rang several times, and he was embarrassed to admit his relief that it hadn't picked up. But then the ringing stopped, and he heard a whisper of memory as her voice filled his ear.

"You on your way?" Millie Sue Jenkins was direct and to the point. It seemed some things never changed.

"I'm in Australia."

"I know. I was the one who called Ivy." That surprised him. He assumed it would have been Mike Paul, the one person in Big Bend he talked to on a regular basis. There was a pause, a quiet that stretched uncomfortably. She wasn't gonna make this easy.

"Millie, I—"

"Just don't come through the front doors of the hospital. We all know you like to cause a ruckus, but this isn't the time."

The line went dead, and he stared at it for a good long while. Long enough for the engines to ramp up as the plane began to taxi down the runway. Once they were in the air, he tucked the phone back into his pocket and tried not to think about home and Bent and the ranch. About his dad and all that pain and regret.

Mostly, he tried not to think about Millie—hell, he tried real hard—but as the plane sliced through the blinding sunlight, it wasn't Sydney Harbor that filled his view. It was auburn hair, sky-blue eyes, and cinnamon freckles that kissed the bridge of a nose he knew better than his own. It was a mouth made for sin or singing or pretty much every fantasy he'd ever had as a young buck. A mouth that used to smile for him.

But that all ended the day he left, and he was pretty sure hell would freeze over before he saw her light up again. At least, not for him.

"Shit," he muttered. He'd really made a mess of things. He closed his eyes somewhere over the Pacific Ocean and fell into a deep, troubled sleep. He had no way of knowing about the storm he was headed into, because if he had, he might have turned the damn plane around and stayed as far away from Montana as he could. Sent his well wishes to Bent and offered whatever he could from a remote location.

But fate had a way of playing hard with those who leave carnage in their wake, even when they don't mean to. For those touched by the sun and good fortune and the kind of things Cal took for granted. She had a way of saying, *Time's up, buddy, it's your turn to deal.*

And for Cal Bridgestone, that time was now. He just didn't know it yet.

CHAPTER 2

Millie Sue Jenkins woke up before the sun was anywhere near the horizon. She rolled out of bed, stubbed her toe on the night table, and let loose some colorful language as she limped out to the kitchen. After a grumpy hello to Mr. Higgins, the overly fat, overly needy cat she'd adopted two years earlier, she attempted to wake up. Millie wasn't a morning person by anyone's definition—in fact, she was about as far from Miss Sunshine as her butt was from the moon—so it meant she had to try extra hard on a day like this.

She needed to be on her toes, so to speak. She took her time and downed three cups of strong brewed java, the kind that put hair on your chest if it mattered and sometimes even if it didn't. Then she made herself a bunch of scrambled eggs, which she pushed around on her plate more than she ate. As the first rays of sunlight began to break open the night sky, she walked into an ice-cold shower. On purpose. *For fifteen minutes.*

Millie felt she owed it to the general public to at least try to get her shit together before she greeted the day properly.

Because the fact of the matter was, her current mental state was cause for concern for a few reasons: a general lack of energy by midday, and a decided lack of enthusiasm for the pile of laundry that covered half her bedroom floor. But truthfully, the fact that she wasn't exactly a nice person to be around was probably number one. Made worse by all the things she was trying so hard not to think about.

"I'll try to be nice," she said to Mr. Higgins as she ran her fingers through her damp ends. They were tangled something fierce and fell over her shoulder.

Dressed in faded jeans and a simple black T-shirt, she grabbed the blow dryer and leaned against the wall as she began the long process of drying her hair. Wasn't her fault she was addicted to *Criminal Minds* and *Gilmore Girls*, two shows that ran continuously in syndication (and yes, she'd been made aware on multiple occasions that they were polar opposites of each other, but whatever, she liked what she liked). She'd seen each series in its entirety more than once. In fact, she could quote dialogue and such, which, for a show like *Gilmore Girls*, was quite impressive. So more often than not, the flickering light from the television played scenes across the wide expanse of windows of the living room until well into the early morning.

Hence the need for strong java.

And the sleeping in until at least nine a.m., which her job running the Sundowner allowed.

But not today. She grimaced and tossed the blow dryer back onto the counter. *Nope, not today*. She considered gathering up the clothes on the floor for all of five seconds (who was she kidding, laundry wasn't a strong suit) and then walked over them and headed back to the kitchen, her mind already on something else.

She rinsed out her coffee mug and set it on the counter

to dry, then moved to the large living room window. It was bright out there, a robin's-egg-blue sky as far as you could see, and it took a minute for her eyes to adjust to the glare so she could have a look at the first significant snowfall of the season. Her place was up on a hill that fell away to the road below and then rolled up the other side into a small valley. In the distance, the Rockies were picture-postcard snow-capped beauties, same as always. They never failed to lift her spirits.

She'd bought this place free and clear after her father had passed four years ago, leaving her a sizable inheritance. There wasn't a day that went by that she didn't thank him. It had been a dark time, and this gift meant more than he could have known, independence being the main one. Millie Sue wasn't beholden to a soul, and never would be.

She dragged her gaze from the window and exhaled slowly. Today wasn't the day to be hanging on to the ghosts of her past.

The snow had come fast, and it was staying, three feet deep from the looks of it on either side of the driveway. With a sigh, she reached for the long puffer coat hung by the door and slipped it on while angling into her Kodiak boots. She laced them up good and tight, pulled a hat over her hair and gloves on her hands, and headed out to shovel the porch. Treat Daniels had been by hours earlier and made a couple of passes of the driveway with his rig, so that was fine, but she had about forty-five minutes of elbow grease before the porch and walkway were cleared.

The sun was shining down on that million-dollar view. If it was any other day, Millie would be content. Happy. Whistling a tune and singing to the wilderness. But nothing about this day was normal or good or anything like the other three hundred and nineteen days before it.

And to think she'd had such high hopes for the year, way back in January when things were new and fresh and the only Bridgestones who mattered, Bent and Ryland, were in her life. Who knew that by mid-November, it would all be for nothing. Because even though she'd gotten good news the night before about Bent, the fact that in less than a few hours Cal would be home made her twitchy. Hell, twitchy wasn't the right word for it, but she didn't want to verbally give the ball of nerves in her stomach anything better.

It pissed her off that she felt anything after all this time.

Millie decided not to think about Cal or Ivy, or anyone connected to him, until she had to. And really, for all she knew, Millie was worrying over nothing. Once Cal found out that Bent would be okay eventually, that his brain was functioning like it should and all his limbs were intact, he'd probably hop back on that big old plane of his and disappear as quick as he'd come.

Cal was good at that. Disappearing into the night without a word. Without so much as a...

"Cut it out, Mills," she muttered as she tossed the last shovel full of snow over the railing. She squinted into the distance at the mountain range that disappeared into snow-heavy clouds, at the forests that fell away from the mountains and all that was between there and her place, and then to a slow-moving vehicle coming up the hill, a large black Chevy. She recognized it and, with the first smile of the day touching the corners of her mouth, pulled off her hat and shook out her long, wavy hair. The air was cold, but not terrible, and she'd gotten warm with all that shoveling.

When the truck pulled into her driveway, she leaned against the railing and waited. Within moments, the door opened, and Mike Paul appeared, an easy grin on his face as he walked toward her. Long legs made quick work of the distance, and he paused at the bottom of her porch. His dark eyes glittered from beneath the brim of his faded Yankees ball cap, and the lower half of his face was covered in a thick, though neatly trimmed, beard. His hair, on the long side, peeked out from the hat and curled around his coat collar. He was a handsome guy, no doubt about it, and the fact of the matter was, Mike Paul knew it. The man had been born with movie-star looks, a smile that didn't quit, and the kind of charm that could make a woman lose her clothes faster than a bottle of tequila. There was a trail of broken hearts in Big Bend to prove it.

"You had your coffee yet?" he asked.

"Three cups."

"You got any more in there?"

"No, but I can put on a pot."

"Sounds good."

Mike Paul followed her into the big cabin and took a seat at the kitchen counter while she brewed up another pot. She'd known him her whole life, and, along with Cal and Ivy, they'd been inseparable. But over the last few years, after Cal left and took Ivy with him, she and Mike Paul had gotten closer. There was a time she thought he would come to mean more to her, but one night after closing time and too much Jack and Coke, a disastrous kiss had let them both know there were no romantic strings pulling them together. No, sir. Millie Sue was attracted to a different kind of poison.

Cal Bridgestone.

"They're back." His voice was low, and she froze, glancing over her shoulder. "About an hour ago. I saw the plane on the private runway outside of Bozeman."

"There are lots of private planes coming into Bozeman every day." She kept her voice light as she measured out the grinds.

"Yeah, but they don't have a bull on the side."

"A bull?"

Mike nodded and made a gesture with his hands. "Big one. Dangling a gold record from its......"

She turned around and raised an eyebrow.

"Horns," Mike replied with a grin.

"God, he's so..." Anger punched through her as she waited for the coffee to brew. Irritated with herself, Millie took a few seconds and then exhaled. She shouldn't be mad about a damn bull on the side of a plane. *I shouldn't feel anything.*

Which was why she was mad. When would the day come that she felt nothing? She crossed over to the cupboard and grabbed two new mugs.

"He's so...?" Mike Paul prompted.

"So...so full of himself." The words exploded like bullets erupting from her chest.

"I suppose if you sell as many records as Cal does, you'd have a bull on the side of your private plane too."

"Downloads."

"Huh?"

"They don't really count records anymore. It's all digital and downloads and streaming."

"I thought vinyl was on the comeback."

"Maybe for the kids who fancy themselves to be retro."

"You have a player in the living room."

"It's an antique." She poured his cup and set it in front of him. "But I fancy myself retro."

Mike accepted a mug full of strong black coffee and sat back on his stool, his gentle smile all but gone. "You okay?"

"Of course, I'm okay."

"You look like you've been up for hours." Millie's expression would shut up most men, but Mike Paul wasn't most men. “This can’t be easy for you.” He knew the history more than anyone.

“You shouldn’t be okay either,” Millie countered. “I wasn’t the only one he left.”

“There’s a big difference between you and me,” Mike said quietly. “I always knew he was gonna leave. Hell, we talked about it a lot. And I—” He stopped abruptly, and she set down her mug, in the mood to fight.

“What?” Her tone was argumentative. She rested both palms on the counter and moved directly in front of him.

“Nothing.”

“Say it,” she ground out, anger building from deep inside, so hot and heavy, her words felt acidic. “Tell me what you were going to say, Mike Paul. Or so help me God, I’ll—”

“Kill me with your coffee mug?”

“People have been killed with less.”

“You’re not wrong.” Mike took a long drink and emptied his mug. He glanced up at her, and she saw the worry. “Cal and I are good. Always have been. We talk, you know that. But you’re still in love with him.”

Her mouth opened, the denial hard and flat, but it never left her tongue because what was the point? She’d loved Cal Bridgestone for as long as she had memory. Every milestone in her life had Cal in it. First trail ride. First skinny-dip in the pond. First kiss. First fight. *First everything*. And for a time, he’d loved her right back. Until he didn’t. Until something meant more to him than her heart.

Millie Sue, cursed as she was, couldn’t turn off her feelings no matter how hard she tried. No matter the distance between them or the mountain of hurt that filled it all up.

It was barely noon by now, and this day was already headed well into the toilet because Mike Paul was right. She was still in love with Cal Bridgestone and probably would be until the day she drew her last breath. It was how she was built. She had one heart, and she'd given it away a long time ago. The problem being it was never given back.

The house was silent as she rinsed and then put away their coffee mugs, then topped up Mr. Higgins's food dish. She had errands to run and an early shift at the Sundowner, the place she co-owned with her cousin Zach. She'd also agreed to pick up little Nora from school and bring her back to the Sundowner, where she was to meet Vivian Bridgestone, who would take the little girl back to the ranch, or wherever it was Vivian was staying. She was a cool cucumber and not exactly on speaking terms with her family.

Seriously, there wasn't a more screwed-up family in the region. Probably the country.

Her mood brightened a bit at the thought of Nora, who was, in fact, a little angel put on this earth by God in the midst of the Bridgestone storm. There wasn't a sweeter child in all of Montana. Another Bridgestone who'd stolen her heart on sight.

She locked up and gave Mike Paul a quick kiss on the cheek. He'd taken over the family business, a veterinary clinic outside Big Bend, and was on his way to several calls in the area.

"I'll see you later," he said. And he would. Like most singles in Big Bend, their evenings ended up at the Sundowner.

With a soft smile, she waved him away and got into her Silverado. It took longer to get to town because of the snow, and for the rest of the day, Millie found herself one step behind. Which, in and of itself, was a welcome distraction because it didn't give her a lot of time to think. She grabbed the items on the list Zach had left the night before, dropped them off at the Sundowner, and then took her truck in for service, which was delayed because they were short on mechanics. By the time she got to Big Bend Elementary school to pick up Nora, she had exactly one minute to spare.

She nodded to the other moms, most of them women she'd gone to school with, and did her best to keep a scowl from her face when Mary Margaret Christchurch headed over. The woman was the biggest gossip in town and no doubt angling for information about Bent and the accident, and Daisy Mae. The woman sucked the energy out of everything she touched, and Millie braced for impact.

"Oh my Gawd, Millie. How awful is it that Bent's just hanging on by a thread? Why, I heard it's been nothing but touch and go since they brought him in." The woman didn't give Millie a chance to respond or correct her very wrong assumption. "I also hear that Cal's back in town." Her features changed, subtly, but it was enough for Millie's body to tighten. "That must be hard for you." It wasn't a question, so Millie didn't feel a need to answer. She said nothing, and when Mary Margaret opened her mouth to spew more dirt, she was saved when Nora ran out and pushed right by the nosy woman.

"Miss Millie!" Her young, girlish voice was full of glee as she launched herself into Millie's arms. Millie bundled her up into the big truck and didn't give Mary Margaret another thought. What was the point? People like that would talk and gossip and fill in the holes with their own story.

Once they were settled, little Nora chatted away about the big butterfly she'd painted in class, and she'd just finished the very descriptive story when Millie turned onto Dry Lake Road. It didn't take long to cross town on account it was home to barely eight thousand souls.

"Here we are, kiddo." Millie parked her truck in the

same spot she'd had since she was a teenager and grabbed Nora's pink unicorn backpack. "Your Auntie Viv is gonna take care of you."

Nora's big brown eyes were soft, and she scrunched up her face. "Am I gonna see Daddy today?" Her voice was high, and Millie thought she detected a bit of a tremble beneath the words.

"I don't know, honey, but if not today, then I bet real soon."

"Auntie tolded me last night his booboos were better."

"They are." She guided the little girl with her hand and walked into the bar via the back entrance. Then traipsed through the kitchen, yelling out hellos to big George Caplan the cook and Sharon, a waitress who'd been at the Downer longer than Millie could remember. After bypassing the office and the washrooms, they walked into a large open room with a stage directly in the center with tables scattered around it. The bar lined the entire left side, and a dance floor sat at the far end. Zach appeared from nowhere. If Millie had been paying attention, she would have noticed the sheen of sweat on his face and the nervous tic on the right side of his mouth.

As it was, she was focused on navigating her way past all the tables with a little girl in tow, a fully stuffed backpack and lunch pail, as well as a box of supplies for behind the bar.

"Hey," Zach said quickly.

"Sorry I'm late." She shoved the box into his arms and then moved past, Nora's little mittened hand tucked into her own. "I've been running to catch up all day. And I—"

"You look like my Daddy."

Millie almost tripped over her own feet and stopped in her tracks. Her eyes were glued to the floor on account of the whole nearly-tripping-over-her-feet thing, and as she brought then up slowly, her stomach sank to where her eyes had been.

Scuffed boots. Long, jean-clad legs. Thick blue plaid button-up over a white T-shirt. Hair that waved over said plaid collar. Wide shoulders. Strong jaw with a couple of days of growth. Beat-up Buffalo Bills cap. Pale eyes with a whisper of gray.

Cal Bridgestone in the Sundowner. The one place she never expected him to be. An image of that last night together momentarily blurred her vision. Of him standing in nearly the same spot. The air electric with anger and passion and a whole bunch of other things. She remembered her words and wondered if he did too.

His eyes gave nothing away as he stared at her silently, and all she could think was that hell, indeed, had frozen over.

CHAPTER 3

CAL HAD ARRIVED IN MONTANA EXACTLY SIX HOURS AGO, AND in that time, a lot happened. After the plane refueled and jetted to Nashville with the rest of his team, Ivy drove him to the hospital.

"You're not coming in with me?"

"No." Ivy glanced away. "I don't do well in hospitals, and besides, I think you and Bent are better off without an audience. I've got some things to take care of but I'll be in touch." She paused and glanced back at him as he slid out of the rental. "A piece of advice?"

"Sure."

"Stay away from Millie Sue."

He didn't bother with a reply, and Ivy obviously wasn't expecting one. The window rolled back up, and she sped away. He thought of Millie's advice the day before and decided it was solid. Cal avoided the front doors and snuck in the back way, near the cafeteria.

Big Bend Trauma Center was small, though well-equipped, and it didn't take long for him to spy someone he knew: Mackenzie Fischer. She was a couple of years older than Cal and, wearing a white lab coat, with a stethoscope slung around her neck, he guessed she was a doctor. Something she confirmed when she spied him and, after chatting with a nurse, made her way over.

Her inky black hair was pulled into a ponytail that emphasized high cheekbones and a generous mouth. With light blue eyes and golden-brown skin, she was a study in contrasts. Her genetics were no different from a lot of locals —her mother's family were Crow, and her father was a tall strapping man of Nordic descent whose forefathers had come to Montana on the wagon trail nearly one hundred and fifty years ago.

"Cal," she said warmly. "It's been a minute."

"More like ten." He cracked a smile he didn't feel. "At least." He cleared the cobwebs from his throat and didn't waste any time. "Where is he?"

"Follow me," she said, pointing at the elevators. "I was just on my way up. I'm sure you've heard the news."

His stomach clenched at her words, and Cal did his best to hold himself together. "News?" Even so, his voice sounded thin and weak in his ears.

"Bent's doing very well, all considering. A bit of a miracle, and we don't mind those around here. The last few years have been rough."

As he followed her into the elevator, relief washed over him. His throat was so damn tight, he couldn't speak.

Mack pressed the third-floor button and gave him a reassuring smile. "Your brother is a strong man. I wasn't sure how he'd be looking three days ago. He has two broken ribs, a broken leg, and we had to remove his spleen. He also had a serious myocardial contusion."

At Cal's confused look, she offered a soft smile. "A bruised heart. However, it was the swelling in his brain that concerned me the most. We had to remove part of his scalp to alleviate the pressure, which is normal procedure, don't worry about that. But like I said..." She stepped off the elevator and he followed suit. "He's strong, he has a lot to fight for, and he wants to live. The swelling went down much more quickly than I'd anticipated. Last night, we did a CT and an MRI. After a thorough examination, I'm fairly confident he'll make a complete recovery. This isn't going to be overnight. He's definitely got a long road ahead of him, but he's lucky. It could have been a lot worse."

"He's lucky and stubborn as hell."

"Aren't all the Bridgestones?"

They reached the end of the hall. Cal was so intent on Mack's words, he didn't notice that every single person on the floor had stopped to look. It wasn't until Mackenzie glanced over his shoulder and raised an imperious eyebrow that he realized he was under scrutiny.

"Don't mind them. It's not often a bona fide superstar walks onto this ward." She nodded. "Here we are."

Mackenzie pushed open the last door on the left, and they entered a large, private room. There were no flowers or balloons or cards. The blinds were half drawn, allowing a small sliver of light that didn't do much. There was a bed with a bunch of blinking machines surrounding it, and a beat-up-looking guy in the middle. Bent's right leg was in a cast. His head was swathed in bandages. His face was puffy and black and blue. Yet even in that state, there was no mistaking the strong Bridgestone lines.

"He's on some pretty heavy-duty pain meds and has been sleeping a lot, which is good, so I can't tell you when he'll wake up, but you're more than welcome to stay until he does. Can I get you anything?" She was looking at the machines and making notes on her tablet.

"I'm good."

"Okay. I have rounds but will check in later. If you need anything, just pull that rope over the bed and I'm sure the nurses will come running like gazelles." She chuckled and took two steps back. "Oh, wait. I have a letter for you. I'll be right back. It's at the nurse's station."

She disappeared before Cal had a chance to say anything, but was back moments later, a crisp white envelope with his name scrawled across it in hand. Mackenzie gave it to him and, with a wink, was gone. A glance told him that it was written by his sister Vivian. He recognized the loopy penmanship instantly. He opened it. The words inside were few, but the message was clear.

I WAS TOLD you were coming back, so I've decided to leave town early. I know you'll look after little Nora, because despite what most folks think, I know you're a good man. Also, you owe this family. I can't be here right now. It's too long a story to tell. Ryland needs some guidance. Who knows if Scarlett will show up, and Bent will need time to heal. Pick up Nora at the Sundowner after school. Millie was grabbing her. I've told Bent, and he's good with this.

Viv

PS. Don't screw this up.

CAL READ THE NOTE TWICE, the words blurring the second time around. This is what his family was. Scattered like fall leaves, pulled thin by time and pain. And the thing of it was, he couldn't be mad at his sister—he'd cut and run years ago and never came back. But little Nora? What the hell did he know about looking after a little girl? He'd never even met her. Then there was Millie Sue. The past, it seemed, was gunning for him, and he didn't have the tools to stop it.

More tired than he was willing to admit, he plopped onto the chair by his brother's bedside and stayed there for a couple of hours until he gave up hope that Bent would actually wake. Cal was running on zero sleep and a whole lot of worry, thinking a cup of coffee or a shot of whiskey was what he needed, when Bent's right eye slid open. He tried to speak, but Cal shook his head and scooped the cup of water from the table beside the bed. Gently, he placed a straw between his brother's lips and held it there until Bent stopped drinking. Then he set it down in the exact spot he'd grabbed it from. He took a moment. Gathered his thoughts.

"You look like shit," he said, voice low and rough.

"I feel..." Voice gravelly, his brother worked the muscles in his throat. "Worse than I look," Bent managed to say, the words slow, as if he was taking time to get them right.

For a good long while, the brothers looked at each other in silence. So many things to say and not enough balls to say them. Eventually, Bent swallowed and, after a bit of a struggle, spoke. "How long you here?"

The sentence was short, but loaded with emotion. Cal heard it in the unspoken words that filled the gaps. Five years ago, a different Cal would have searched for a way out. He would have called Ivy and told her to fix this—to hire the best people to look after his family so he didn't have to feel guilty about not doing it himself.

"As long as it takes," he replied softly, surprising himself because he meant every word.

Relief eased the pain on his brother's face, and Bent nodded, wincing again. "Good," he rasped. "Shoulda rolled the truck years ago."

Cal frowned, not sure what he meant.

"Might have brought you back sooner." Exhausted, Bent sank into the bed just as Mackenzie walked back into the room.

All business, she took Cal by the arm. "He needs to rest. Bent might be our miracle, but he's still got a ways to go. I'll let you know how he does tonight, and if all is well, you can maybe bring Nora by tomorrow."

Cal left the hospital the same way he'd come, through the back. Then he walked uptown to the Dodge dealership, glad he'd worn boots and the warm coat Ivy had bought for him while they'd still been in Sydney. Dirk Madison owned the place, a familiar face from his youth, and less than an hour later, he drove off in a brand-new truck that cost a small fortune, a top-of-the-line fully loaded Laramie. It was big and mean and safe. Ten minutes after he left the dealership, Cal was parked at the back of the Sundowner. He cut the engine and sat there for a couple of minutes. He was a confident man. Cocky, some would say. But being back here made him feel off balance. Made the ground feel unsteady.

This was where he began. Him and Millie up on that stage. And this was where it had all gone to hell. He stared across the lot at a building that looked exactly as he remembered, weathered roof a mud gray to match the rest of the place. Then, before he lost his nerve, Cal pulled up his collar and headed inside.

It was dark, the way most honkytonks are, with neon signs and bad artwork on the wall. It smelled of beer and grease and memory, and after sliding onto a stool, he ordered a beer from a young lady tending bar. She was friendly, but with his cap pulled low, he was pretty sure she had no idea who he was—and that was fine with him. He kept his head down, and no one attempted to talk to him.

That was the way it was out here. Folks minded their own business until you made their business yours.

Cal nursed his beer and slowly began to relax. A man joined the girl behind the bar. Something about him looked familiar, but he didn't pay much attention because his thoughts were elsewhere. His brother. The accident. A niece he'd never met.

Millie Sue Jenkins.

He'd thought about this moment many times. Thought of what he'd say. How he'd act. He used to tell himself they were both older and, hopefully, wiser. That the past could stay where it was because they were grown-ups now. They'd moved on. Lived their lives.

Of course, all that sounded good when you were halfway across the world, sucking on a bottle of Jack at three in the morning. But to be here, in this place, none of it felt good or right or even possible.

He noticed the girl tending bar pointing somewhere behind him, and Cal swiveled on his chair, trying to find what she saw. His body hummed with the kind of energy he usually felt just before stepping on a stage in front of thousands of screaming fans, because he knew.

He knew.

Then he saw her walking toward the bar, and the world kind of fell away from him. He didn't realize he'd slipped from his stool until he found himself standing a few feet away. Snowflakes dusted the hat on her head, and her long hair looked darker than he remembered, the ends waving down her shoulders and back. Her skin was still tanned even though it was mid-November, and she was bundled up but good, her entire body swathed in a long black winter coat. Her head was bent, so she hadn't spied him yet. He found himself yearning to see the pair of eyes that had haunted him for years.

The guy who'd been behind the bar stepped in the way. Cal waited, unsure how to proceed. He watched the two of them speak, Millie's face now obscured by the man. Something crept up Cal's body until it settled into his chest. Something dark and maybe a little possessive. Was this Millie's better half? It wasn't inconceivable that she was married. Hell, she'd always had a pack of guys yipping at her heels. He should know. He used to be one of them. But wouldn't Mike Paul have said something?

"Hey, you look like my daddy."

The little singsong voice came from nowhere. His gaze dropped to the little angel at Millie's side. Silvery-blonde pigtails peeked from under a pink Barbie hat, and they framed a cute-as-a-button face that housed big brown eyes and snow-kissed pink cheeks. Her nose was small, her lips like rosebuds, and those eyes, exact replicas of his brother's, looked up at him adoringly.

She was the perfect mashup of Daisy Mae and Bent. A little girl he'd never met because pride and a whole lot of other stuff had gotten in the way.

Her face scrunched up as she cocked her head to the side, studying him intently. She didn't say another word, and, unnerved by the steady gaze of a human less than six years old, Cal dragged his eyes from hers until he met Millie's.

He had no words—they were frozen in his throat. He let himself drink her in, let himself believe this was going to be okay. Her expression was muted at first, but as the seconds ticked by, her eyes began to glitter and color crept across her cheeks—a slow burn, if you like—and her expression changed. It deepened and darkened, and she made no effort to hide her dislike or disdain or whatever the hell it was buried inside her.

"What the *hell* are you doing *here*?" Her voice was like whiskey over ice, rough and sexy all at once. It was the kind of voice that did things to a man. The kind that could cut to the bone. The kind that could excite.

"Miss Millie," Nora said with a squeal. "That's a bad word." Then the little girl looked back at him, eyes older than they should be, fixed and true. "You look like my daddy," she repeated, as if trying to figure out a puzzle.

Cal cleared his throat and bent down so his head was level with the little girl's. "That's because your daddy is my brother."

"Oh." Her little nose wrinkled in confusion. "I thought Uncle Ry is Daddy's brother."

"He is." Cal paused. "And so am I."

The little girl slowly shook her head. "He never tolded me he had another one."

Throat tight, Cal took a moment and then spoke softly. "I've been away." He glanced up at Millie. "But now I'm back."

"For five minutes," she said, enunciating each syllable as if the words tasted like crap.

Cal straightened and slowly shook his head so there was no mistaking his intention. "No," he replied, keeping his voice light. "Should be at least ten."

Millie's eyes flashed. "Thought you were at the hospital with Bent."

"I was."

"Then you know he's all good."

"I do."

"So why are you here? You should be riding that fancy bull all the way back to Australia."

Ah. She'd heard about his private plane. "I think I'm done riding." He flashed a grin, an attempt to make light, but she wasn't biting. "For the next little while, anyway."

"Why are you here?" she repeated, not bothering to hide her irritation or impatience.

"For Nora."

"What?" Her right eyebrow rose so dramatically, it slipped up underneath the edge of her wool hat. "Vivian is picking her up."

"Vivian is on her way back to Alaska." He winked at Nora, who was watching the exchange closely. The air was heavy with the kind of stuff a little girl had no business knowing about. "Uncle Cal is gonna be watching you for the next..." He looked up at Millie. "Ten minutes or so."

Her mouth opened, but nothing came out, which was something of a miracle because Millie Sue Jenkins was rarely at a loss for words. By the time she found her tongue, he had offered his hand to Nora, who'd taken it without hesitation, and was headed for a table next to the stage.

"You're staying in Big Bend." Millie had followed them over. He took the little girl's backpack and hung it off the chair.

"Didn't we just have this conversation?"

"And you're looking after Nora?" The disbelief was strong.

"I am."

"You don't know anything about little girls. Hell, you don't know anything about Nora. What the fuck is Bent thinking?"

"Miss Millie, that is a really bad word." The shock on Nora's face was comical, but the adults weren't paying attention. Her voice dropped to a whisper. "Badder than the S word."

"Where are you staying?" Millie asked.

"The ranch, I guess."

"I give you two days tops." She looked like she had more to say, but then she pursed her lips and remained silent.

Cal shouldn't have been surprised at her attitude. Hell, he'd expected worse if he was being honest with himself. But the fact that she thought he'd abandon a little girl after two days did something to him. It got under his skin and burned. He didn't like the feeling one bit.

"I'm here until Bent doesn't need me anymore."

"We'll see." Millie kissed the top of Nora's head. "Be good for your uncle." Then she turned on a dime and disappeared the way she'd come, leaving him alone with a little girl who'd managed to wiggle out of her pink-and-purple coat. Her pigtails were a static mess of electricity, and she was impatiently trying to brush strands from her face as she looked up at him.

"Are you gonna buy me a milkshake?"

"Whatever you want, darlin'."

"And some french fries and brussels sprouts?"

Cal doffed his jacket and took the seat opposite Nora. "Anyone ever tell you that brussels sprouts and french fries don't go together?"

"Daddy says my tastebuds are special." She giggled, and the sound punched him somewhere between his heart and his head. He was gonna do right by his brother. He owed him that and so much more. Besides, how hard could it be to look after a little kid? She wasn't in diapers and could obviously feed herself.

Cal was feeling pretty damn good about things when, a couple of hours later, he drove through the Triple B gates and, after another twenty minutes or so, parked in front of the large house set up on a small hill that overlooked the barns and outbuildings. The structure had been built in 1935, replacing a smaller bungalow that still stood a couple of hundred yards to the left, back behind a thick stand of pine. The house was antebellum with wide sweeping verandas held in place by thick white columns, floor-to-ceiling windows to let in the natural beauty, and double-wide garden doors. His great-great-grandmother had been a Southern belle, one of the Bodines from New Orleans, and she'd been brought to the wilds of Montana by Joshua Bridgestone.

Looking up at the place was like seeing a memory come alive. Some of it good. A lot of it not so much. It was sobering being back here, and Cal took a moment, heaving a sigh as he turned off the engine. He let Nora out of the truck and grabbed her backpack while she scrambled up the stairs onto the wide veranda. The pathway was shoveled and clear of snow, as were the steps. He made it up three of them before the front door opened, spilling light into the early evening gloom. The figure that stood in the doorway was full of shadow and light, and he squinted in order to see better, but there was no mistaking the frame.

"I swear, Cal Bridgestone, if you don't get up here and give me a big ol' hug, I just might whoop your butt like I done many times before."

For the first time since he'd arrived back in Montana, Cal felt the kind of joy he'd damn near forgot about. He jumped onto the veranda and enveloped Rose Whitehead in a gorilla hug that had the old girl giggling like a teenager. She hugged him back just as fierce. The two of them clung to each other for several seconds before she disengaged herself. The sight of tears in her eyes made him feel like shit, and for a moment, he was silent on account of the big lump in his throat.

It had been too long. And that was on him.

"Hey," he finally managed to say, taking her in. She'd aged, this woman who'd been like a mother to him. Her hair was threaded with silver, her golden-brown skin weathered, deep lines carved onto a proud face. But her dark eyes glittered, and the wide smile was just as warm as he remembered. "You look exactly the same."

"Now I thought I taught you never to tell no lie."

"No," he replied with a grin. "You taught me to always say the right thing. There's a difference."

"Rosie, I have a new uncle." Nora's excited chatter caught both of them, and Cal's gaze slid to the little girl.

"He's not new child," Rose said, stepping aside and shooing Nora inside. "He's just been absent."

"What does absent mean?" Nora slipped out of her jacket and tossed it on the bench just inside the doorway. She didn't wait for an answer and instead whirled around and headed for the stairs.

"Are you coming, Uncle Cal? I want to show you my rabbit. His name is Charlie." She hardly stopped to take a breath and disappeared upstairs, her voice like musical notes that rose and fell.

"She's on a sugar high," Cal admitted sheepishly. "Found I couldn't say no to her."

"She's a Bridgestone through and through. They're all hard to resist." Rose's smile softened as her eyes filled with tears. "She's gonna need you. Nothing like blood when there's a family crisis."

There was no reprimand in her tone. No blaming for all of it. And for that, Cal was grateful.

"Ryland hasn't been home in two days. That boy is going to be the death of me." Rose slipped into her jacket. "I've got two casseroles defrosting in the fridge, and I did a grocery run so you won't have to bother yourself with any of that." She winked. "I'll see you in a couple of days."

"What?" Startled, Cal's eyes widened. "You're not staying?"

"Calvin Strong Bridgestone, I got my own family to take care of. Charlene has three babies now, and with her teaching on the reservation, they take up just about all my time. I'm only helping out because Bent's not here." She reached up and kissed his cheek. "But don't you worry none, I'll be back on Friday to do some cleaning and any laundry you can't get to." She motioned toward the kitchen. "Nora's schedule is on the fridge. She has ballet tomorrow after school, and that girl sure needs the discipline, so don't you forget."

"Ballet?" Visions of tutus and frills and nosy mothers filled his mind. "I thought she'd be riding."

"Oh, she rides. Got her own pony, and she has her chores that she tends to. That's something your brother made sure of. But Bent wanted her to have the best of both worlds, so she does ballet. Check in with Dal. He's living in the foreman's place. Anything that has to do with running this place, he can fill you in on."

She stepped toward the door, a wide smile easing the lines around her mouth. "I know the life you've made for yourself is worlds away from the ranch. And I want you to know how proud we are. All of us. But I'm glad you're here now. I made sure your old room was cleaned and there are fresh sheets on your bed. I'm sure it's not what you're used to, but then whoever said a body needed one-thousand thread count to get a good night's sleep is just plain crazy."

Cal knew firsthand that thread count made a difference, but no way was he arguing with Rosie.

"If you run into problems, give me a call. Number is the

same." Rose put her hand on the doorknob and paused. Her features shifted ever so slightly, and she opened her mouth and then closed it. After a few quiet moments, she spoke. "A lot of things have changed around here, Cal. But a lot have stayed the same. That's the way of it in the valley. It's not my business, and I don't mean to butt in where I don't belong, but while you're here, I'd like to ask two things from you."

Cal shuffled his feet, feeling like the kid she'd caught sneaking whiskey from his daddy's cupboard all those years back. "Anything," he replied carefully.

"Go see your father. He's living out at Blue Ridge in the Founder's Cabin."

That surprised Cal. "He's on the ranch?"

Rose nodded. "And promise you won't get up in Millie's business. That girl has finally found some kind of happiness. I'd hate for you to go and ruin it, because we both know you being here is temporary."

"Rosie, I never meant..." He stumbled over the words, not finding the right ones. Regret had a way of doing that to a person. "I had to leave." They were hollow, but they were all he had.

"It's okay, son," she said quietly, opening the door. "Not everyone or every situation is supposed to be neat and tidy. I know you're not the mean-spirited type." Her eyes softened a bit. "You don't set out to hurt folks. Not on purpose, anyway. You're just not the staying kind, and for most of us, that's what hurts in the end. The fact that you feel the need to leave us while we want you here so bad." She gave a small shrug. "But that could be us being selfish, so don't pay it too much mind."

With that, Rose headed out into the crisp winter air, leaving Cal staring at the door. He was glad Millie had settled into a life that made her happy. The fact that he wasn't a part of it shouldn't matter. Rosie was right. He was the leaving kind.

After a few moments, Cal trudged upstairs, following the still-chattering voice of his niece all the way to the end of the hall. It was much later when a little girl who'd eaten too much sugar finally fell asleep. He tucked her in, dragged his exhausted butt downstairs, and glanced around. The place was in darkness and eerily silent. He stood for a while in the foyer, unsure in a house that had been a home. A place full of memory.

He should go to bed. Get some sleep.

He thought about that for a while, there in the dark, but instead of heading to his room, Cal grabbed a bottle of Jack from the bar and settled onto a chair in the den. He turned off his phone, blown up with hundreds of text messages he had no interest in reading, and kept to the shadows. He decided to get good and drunk so he could forget. Eventually, he got to the point he couldn't drink anymore...but the forgetting...that was something else.

Because the things he wanted to forget were here to stay.

CHAPTER 4

"Where's Uncle Ry?" The singsong voice woke him. Along with the pokes to his chest. And the tug on his nose.

With a groan, Cal eased off the chair and tried to shake the fog from his mind and body. His neck was sore, his back ached, and his arms and legs weren't working too well either. He eyed the empty bottle on the floor with regret. His mouth felt like sawdust and tasted worse, and his head was home to a couple of UFC fighters kicking the crap out of each other.

"Hey." Again with a poke, but this time to his thigh.

He closed his eyes for a few seconds and then opened them slowly, trying to focus. Nora stared up at him, big eyes shiny and questioning, her hair a mess of curls that needed a good brushing. She clutched a raggedy stuffed animal to her chest, a teddy bear from the looks of it, as bright pink as the nightgown she wore.

He let out a long breath. So. Much. Pink. Outside, it was light, but only just, and Cal had no idea what time it was.

"I'm hungry."

The thought of food made him queasy, and he grimaced. "Yeah?" he mumbled, scratching at his chin.

"And Tabitha isn't here."

"Who's that?" he asked, curious.

"She's Daddy's friend." Nora turned in a circle. "Why did you sleep in here?" She didn't wait for him to answer, but glanced up at him with a small frown. "You smell."

The kid was a straight shooter. It was something most Bridgestones were proud of, so he couldn't fault her on it.

"I need a shower," he replied with a shrug.

"But I'm hungry, and Tabitha isn't here, and I don't know where Uncle Ry is, and I can't reach the high cupboard. I mean, I *can* reach it, but I'm not supposed to stand on chairs. The last time I did, I fell and had a big boobie on my elbow and Daddy yelled at Uncle Ry. And then Uncle Ry got mad and yelled back, and they forgot about my frosted flakes, and I had to have toast instead because that's in the bottom cupboard and I don't have to stand on a chair to get that." She inhaled sharply, nearly out of breath, and grinned. "Uncle Ry makes the best breakfast." Her eyes widened, and she did a little dance. "Sometimes, we have breakfast for supper. My favorite is pancakes with whipped cream and honey and strawberries."

"You don't say." He fished out his cell from his back pocket, noting it was just past six a.m. "Tell you what." He pointed to the door and followed Nora out of the office. "Why don't I get you something to eat, and while you're feeding your belly, I'll grab a shower."

"Are you taking me to school?"

"School bus still doesn't make the trip out to the top road?"

"I never been on the school bus before. Daddy always takes me, but he can't no more because he got hurt, and when he can't, Dallas does." She shrugged. "Or Uncle Ry or Tabitha. I like it better when Uncle Ry takes me because he's funny and tells stories. And sometimes he drives really fast." Her grin faded, little nose scrunched up. "Tabitha doesn't like to talk. Not even about my bunny."

"You sure as hell don't stop talking." He didn't realize he'd said the words out loud until Nora giggled.

"Daddy says I was born with words in my mouth."

"He's right about that."

She grinned up at him. "And you said a bad word again."

"Sorry, kiddo. I'll try to keep the bad words to a minimum."

"It's okay." She shrugged. "Daddy says lots of bad words when he thinks I can't hear him. Even the F word."

"F word?" Cal tried not to laugh.

She nodded and whispered. "Friggen."

Something warm bloomed in his chest. Something warm with the potential to grow. She was so like Daisy. He followed Nora down the hall. "I'll take you to school and try to round up Ryland. I'm sure he's not far."

His youngest brother was seventeen, so Cal wasn't too worried, but he supposed if he was in charge now, he needed to at least find out where the kid had spent the night.

The cupboards were well stocked, and his niece had no problem directing him to the box of cereal she liked. He poured out a generous amount, dumped in some milk, and got Nora a glass of orange juice. She set up her bear on the chair beside her and tucked in.

Nora was done by the time he finished up in the shower. After digging through Bent's closet, Cal found a clean pair of jeans and an old Henley that at one time had been black, but was now a faded, dull gray. It was comfortable, but more importantly, it fit. Cal had a couple of inches on his brother, but Bent was broader through the shoulders. The man was built for ranching, but then all the Bridgestones were.

His niece had chosen her own outfit to wear to school. He tried not to smile as she twirled in front of him. He was pretty sure the pink-and-white-striped tights she'd pulled on underneath a brown-and-greed plaid dress didn't exactly match, but the combination sure made his niece happy. Blue cowboy boots rounded out her look, and her long hair was pulled back into two ponytails he'd tried hard to make stick, though the right side drooped and would probably fall out by the time he got her to school. He'd take the win for managing to drag a brush through the curls, while she'd continued talking and waving her hands and moving so much, he was sure she had ants in her pants.

While she was grabbing her coat and the lunch box from the fridge (courtesy of Rose), he scooped up his phone from the office, now fully charged. He scrolled through a bunch of messages he had no intention of answering until later and read a few that caught his attention. Ivy had responded to his message from the day before.

Ivy: *Glad Bent's going to be okay and out of the woods. Don't worry about the last date in Australia. I've already rescheduled for January. I've also got a press release slated for later today, your publicist is in the loop, and the band and crew know as well. I decided to take a few days off. I'll contact you when I'm back.*

Huh. No one deserved a vacation more than Ivy, but her timing couldn't be worse. He thought of the list of things he needed done, things up until this moment he'd assumed she'd do for him, and let out a soft sigh. When the hell had he become that guy? The one who expected shit to get done without lending a hand? It was easy to do, considering most people who circled his planet were nothing but ass-kissers who did more for him than they should. "No" wasn't a word he heard from anyone anymore. Hell, the only person on the planet who'd take the time to tell him when he was being an asshole was Ivy.

And Millie.

Clearing her from his mind as quick as she'd come, Cal continued scrolling. Ryland hadn't replied to his text messages the day before. He sent the kid another one, but it showed undelivered, and he realized his brother's cell was either dead or turned off. With a frown, Cal sent Mike Paul a message, asking him to call when he could.

"I'm ready." Nora stomped her foot impatiently.

Cal gave her a once-over, eyes on her boots. "You sure those boots are good?"

"Uh-huh," she replied with a big smile. "They're my favorite, and Daddy lets me wear them to school every single day."

Figuring they must be lined, Cal shoved his cell into his back pocket, and they headed outside. The sun was bright and the air crisp as he shepherded the little girl to his truck. The long driveway had been plowed sometime in the night. He was about to hop in the vehicle when he noticed a man heading his way. Bundled up in a thick sheepskin coat overtop lined coveralls, he was a monster in size, shoulders as wide as his legs were long. Dark curly hair peeked out from underneath a thick wool hat, while his strong jawline was covered in an impressive beard. Dallas Henhawk, their foreman. A few years older than Bent. They'd all grown up on the ranch, with generations before doing the same. He was part of the family, and Cal was happy to see him. His face broke out in a wide grin.

"Long time," Dal said with a slow nod, his steel-blue

eyes settling on Cal. As always, Dallas was a man of few words.

"Too long. I'm sorry for that." Cal cleared his throat. "It's good to see you." He offered his hand, but was pulled into a bear hug.

When the men eventually parted, Dal spoke first. "You don't need to say sorry, Cal. We all know it's a hard job being a bona fide country star." He chuckled, though the mirth slowly left his face. "We're just glad you're here."

Throat suddenly thick, Cal cleared it and nodded to the truck. "I'm taking Nora to school, and then I need to figure out where the hell Ry is." He paused. "You wouldn't happen to know what he's been up to?"

"Haven't a clue. He's been off on his own a lot lately. A girl, I figure." Dal winked. "He's a good kid. A little on the wild side like his brothers were at that age. But he generally stays out of trouble. There's not a lot for him to do here with winter on the way, so I don't see him as much as in the spring and summer." The man's face gentled. "I wouldn't worry too much. All you Bridgestones eventually find your way back home. Some just take longer than others." He took a step back. "You know where I am in the evenings. Stop by and I'll fill you in on the ranch."

"Everything okay?"

"We're fine. Bent's done a good job." He held Cal's gaze. "You been to see the old man yet?"

Surprised at the question, Cal took a few moments. Why was everyone pushing him toward his father? "I don't know. We'll see." His answer was vague, but it was all he had. "When did he move out to Blue Ridge?"

"A couple of years back."

Cal let that information settle. The Founder's Cabin was up on the other side of the valley, tucked beneath a ridge overlooking a creek. It had been the first structure built by a Bridgestone nearly one hundred and fifty years ago. Cal had no idea it was habitable. "I thought hell would freeze over before Bent let him back onto Bridgestone land."

"A lot of things have changed."

"No shit," he muttered to himself. He looked at Dallas. "I'll swing by later for a proper catch-up."

"Sure thing." Dallas back away and, with a nod, turned toward the barns.

Cal hopped into the truck and headed to town. The drive was easy, but halfway there, he turned off the radio on account of Nora's chatter pretty much drowning out anything but her voice. Once at the school, he managed to get her inside without too much fuss. Nora's teacher was none other than Mrs. Smith, the same he'd had all those years ago, and after eyeing up the blue cowboy boots his niece wore, she looked at Cal and shook her head, an easy smile on her face.

"Let's make sure Nora has on her winter boots tomorrow." The reprimand was light, but still... Cal shot an accusatory look at his niece. The little girl paid him no mind as she ran to her cubby.

"That one has more charm in her pinky than anyone I know. Those are her favorite boots. She wore them every day last year." Mrs. Smith paused. "Don't let her run roughshod over you, Calvin. She might look like an angel, and for the most part, she is. But she's also a Bridgestone, and we both know how headstrong you all are." She gave him a big hug and said to give Benton her best wishes, then disappeared into the classroom.

Cal called Ryland's cell *again* and, when he didn't pick up, headed over to the high school. Classes were already in session, so he slipped inside, gave a quick wave to Davis, the same security guard who'd been there when he used to haunt the place, and then made his way to the office.

He spied Mrs. Crabtree at her desk. She glanced up when he entered, pushing her round glasses higher onto her nose. She rose to her feet with a wide smile.

"My goodness. Calvin Bridgestone." She rounded her desk until she stood a few inches away. "I've been wondering if you'd be coming home." Her smile fell a bit. "We were all so sorry to hear about Benton's accident. But I do hear he's on the mend." She winked. "My nephew is a nurse there at the hospital and told me the good news while I was in line at the Coffee Pot."

"That place still standing?"

"I swear it will survive the apocalypse." She waited a beat. "What can I do for you?"

"I was hoping to talk to Ryland. I got into town yesterday, and I'm trying to get organized and all, but I haven't connected with him just yet." He offered a hopeful smile. "Would it be possible to have him called down to the office? Just so I can square away a few things."

"Why, I'd love to help you, Calvin, but Ryland's been absent for a few days now. We all just assumed he was at the hospital."

"Is that so," he answered slowly, feeling a twinge of unease for the first time. "You're probably right. I bet that's where he is. I'll head on over now."

Once he was in his truck, he called Mackenzie, but the doctor hadn't seen Ryland since the day Bent had been brought in. Filing that information away, he asked after his brother and was told to stop by later in the afternoon since she'd just had him taken down for a few more X-rays. She assured him Benton was doing well and ended the call.

Cal stared down at his cell, pondering his next move.

The headache was still there, those UFC fighters headed to extra rounds, when he finally pulled out of the parking lot. He called Mike Paul again, but same as last, there was no answer. With a curse, he gripped the steering wheel as he headed down Main Street. He was nearly to the end of town when he swung a hard right and drove into the parking lot of the Sundowner. Mostly empty, there were a few trucks here and there, ones whose owners had been smart enough to get a ride home the night before. He pulled alongside a small red compact car near the back entrance and hopped out of his truck.

The back door was unlocked, and he strode inside, gaze on a large man chopping onions in the kitchen. Hank Williams fell from the old radio propped at the end of the workspace, and the man hummed along to a song about a good-lookin' woman cookin' up a world of heartbreak.

Cal cleared his throat and offered a smile at the startled look he received. "Sorry to bother you, but I was looking for Millie Sue."

The man's mouth fell open as his eyes widened hilariously. "It's true," he whispered. "You're back. You're really here."

This was the part that always made Cal feel uncomfortable. The recognition. The worship. Folks looked at him like he was some sort of god, when he was the furthest thing from it. He was only a man who liked to write songs and play guitar. He shoved his hands into the pockets of his jeans and hunched his shoulders. "Do you know when she's gonna be in?"

The man wiped his hands on the front of his apron. "Millie is off today."

"Does she still live upstairs?"

"No." The man rounded the corner. "I'm a huge fan.

That acoustic show you did at the Opry was something else." He grabbed a notebook from the counter. "Hey, do you think I could get an autograph?"

"Sure," Cal said, taking the offered pen and pad.

"My name's George Caplan." He inched closer. "If you don't mind using my last name so's folks believe me." He ran his stubby fingers over a hairnet that barely managed his hair. "Bad day for me to forget my cell phone at home. Maybe we could get a selfie some other time?"

"Some other time," Cal murmured. He scribbled his name, then handed back the pad. "Can you tell me where Millie's at?" He asked the question lightly, hoping the man in front of him didn't know the details of their history.

"She bought the old Fenton place at the top of Big Creek Road. It overlooks the valley. Last spread up there with a big old porch. You can't miss it."

He knew exactly where it was. Cal backed away and gave a small wave. "Thanks."

He hopped back in his truck and checked his phone. Still no response from Ryland. Cal thrummed his fingers across the top of the steering wheel for a good two minutes and frowned. He knew Millie had no desire to see him. She'd made that pretty damn clear. And he knew if he went over to her place, there was a fifty-fifty chance she'd try to run him off with a shotgun. And if she didn't do that, he knew there'd be arguing and yelling and maybe some throwing. It was what they did.

But as he headed out to Big Creek Road, he supposed there was a part of him that wanted all that friction. He wanted her to put him in his place. In fact, he deserved it.

Besides, when was the last time anyone pushed back where he was concerned? Said no or told him he was being ridiculous? Not a one. At least, no one since Millie or Bent.

Not that he wanted Millie to toss him on his ass before he found out where the hell Ryland was at. But he had to at least try. And the way Cal saw it, she was his best chance. The Sundowner was the epicenter of Big Bend, and anything worth knowing was heard at that bar.

So, even though he knew showing up at her door was a bad idea, he kinda felt it was his only option.

He just hoped like hell Millie saw things the same way.

CHAPTER 5

Millie Sue was deep in dreamland when persistent pounding managed to worm its way inside her head and wake her up. With a groan, one eye slid open, and she spied Mr. Higgins proudly cleaning his nether regions on the pillow beside her.

"Really?" she said, voice like sandpaper.

The cat paused for all of two seconds, lifted his left leg higher, a fuck-you if she ever saw one, and got back to work. God, it was too early for this. A glance at the clock on the bedside table told her it was nearly nine thirty, and while that was late morning for most folks in these parts, it was not the case for Millie. She'd closed the bar the night before, and once home, made her way through more than her fair share of bourbon while singing and playing the guitar to no one but the cat.

The drinking she'd blame on Cal Bridgestone. The man brought out nothing but the worst in her. But the singing was what she did. She sang when she was happy. Or excited. Or confused. Or sad. She pictured Cal and made a face. She definitely sang when she was annoyed.

Millie frowned and rolled out of bed, then stumbled toward the hallway because the pounding on her front door was an ongoing situation that wasn't stopping. It was probably Mike Paul, and man, she was going to give it to him.

Her bedroom was in darkness on account of the thick blinds she'd installed the day she moved in, but the rest of the house was awash in the kind of brilliant sunshine that bounced off the snow outside and zipped through the windows, nearly blinding her as she emerged from the cave she slept in.

She caught a glimpse of herself in the mirror that was hung on the wall near the kitchen and grimaced. Her hair was a wild mess that was going to take some effort to get through in the shower, and the circles under her eyes told the tale of the night before. She needed water badly, but decided to deal with Mike Paul first.

She should have peeked outside before answering the door, because she would have noticed the truck parked behind hers. A brand-spanking-new truck that belonged to no one she knew, because no one she knew spent over one hundred grand on a tricked-out set of wheels. But because she wasn't thinking clearly, on account of the door banging and the bourbon, she reached for the handle and yanked open the door. "Jesus, stop with the noise. You know I'm not a morning—"

Cold air hit her square in the face and wind whistled around the tall man who stood in front of her. A tall male who was definitely not Mike Paul. She had to blink a few times to rid the sunshine from her eyes, and when she was finally able to focus, Millie noticed Cal's eyes were nowhere near her own but had traveled lower.

Much lower.

She didn't have to look down to know she was barely

dressed. Heck, she was a simple girl, and if she wasn't sleeping naked, she was wearing...

"Still like Minnie Mouse, I see."

His voice was low, intimate. It set off all kinds of things inside her. Hot things. Electric things. *Angry things*. It was the angry things Millie decided to concentrate on, because the angry things would keep her out of trouble.

"What are you doing here?" She poked him in the chest.

"I need to talk to you," he replied, inching closer even as she took a step back.

"Who the hell had the balls to tell you where I live?"

"Come on, Mills. I get you're not too happy I'm here, but don't blame the guy who told me."

She closed her eyes and tried for that place of calm she knew was buried inside her somewhere. It was gonna take a minute, but she could do it. She'd been practicing.

"What guy?"

"What are you going to do to him?" Cal asked softly.

"Kill him," Millie replied without missing a beat, opening her eyes once more and hoping like hell the shit going inside her body wasn't showing up on her face.

"That might cause you some problems."

"I'll decide if it's a problem or not." She grimaced. "What. Guy?"

A ghost of a smile played around the corners of Cal's mouth, and Millie clenched her teeth. God, he was so sure of himself.

"Well, if you can do without a cook, I suppose you could kill him."

"Caplan," she all but spat.

Cal nodded. "George."

She should have known. The man was Cal's biggest fan,

and he'd nearly had a heart attack when one of the servers told him Cal Bridgestone was back in town.

"Idiot," she muttered. That ghost of a smile on Cal's face widened a bit more, but she had his number. She knew all too well the power he held over women. There was no denying it; he'd been born with an overabundance of charm. Heck, she'd fallen for it same as the rest. But she'd learned her lesson, learned it but good, and no way was she falling for his crap again.

She squared her shoulders. Millie Sue Jenkins might still be in love with Cal Bridgestone, but she also disliked him more than any person on the planet. His weapons were useless. He could smile all he damn well pleased.

"I don't have the time or the patience for you, Calvin. Just say whatever it is you came to say and leave me alone."

"You look like shit."

Okay, that wasn't what she'd expected to hear. And was his grin wider?

She clenched her hands. "You drove all the way out here to tell me I look like shit?"

"No," he drawled, "just an observation is all."

"Well, you don't look so good yourself," she shot back. She noted the bloodshot eyes and the shadows beneath them. Cal might smell good, but he was running on empty.

"I had a late night." Cal shifted his feet, gaze falling from hers. "It was..." He paused as if searching for the right words. "It was weird being back there. Without Bent."

She didn't know what to say to that, so Millie remained silent. And vigilant. She needed to be sharp so as to avoid the charm that simmered beneath the surface.

"Could we do this inside? I promise I won't stay long. But you look like you need some coffee, and I could use a cup."

"You expect me to make you a coffee?" The man was unbelievable.

"No," he replied gently. "I'll make the coffee while you shower and..." His eyes dropped to her chest area. "Get into some warmer clothes."

She didn't have to follow his gaze to know her nipples poked out like two headlights in the dark.

"Eyes above my chest," she ground out. Millie realized that Cal wasn't leaving until he said what he wanted to say. She turned on her heel and marched back into her house. She disappeared down the hall to her room without another word and slammed her bedroom door shut. It was a bit dramatic, but she couldn't help herself.

Cal Bridgestone still pushed every single button she owned, and it was going to take more than a hot shower to make it go away. But at the moment, that was her only option. She took her time, shampooed her hair twice, and decided it was as good a time as any to get the razor out and clear away the weeks' worth of hair on her legs. By the time she'd combed out her hair and left it to hang down her back in a wet rope, pulled on an old pair of sweatpants that were two sizes too big along with the matching sweatshirt, she'd been closed up in her bedroom for nearly forty-five minutes.

As she opened the door, she thought that maybe, if she was lucky and every single god that had ever lived was looking down on her, he'd be—

"I didn't leave on you, if that's what you were wondering."

Millie hid a scowl and schooled her features into some semblance of calm as she followed the heavenly scent of coffee out to her kitchen. Cal leaned against the island, his gaze on the window. Her eyes found him immediately and lingered on his strong profile. That old familiar tug had her insides a mess, and she looked away, unhappy with the power he held. She needed to think of the other things, the dark things between them, and then she'd be okay.

"You still have the Martin."

The guitar was lying where she'd left it the night before, on the sofa to their right. It was a beat-up, well-used acoustic, with delicate pearl inlay and a fret board that didn't quit. Cal had given it to her one hot summer night, the day after her seventeenth birthday. And she'd given him so much more.

"I do," she said, clearing her throat a bit as she blinked away the memory. "What's so important you came all the way out here?" She grabbed a cup from the cupboard and poured herself a coffee. She added cream and two sugars, and when she had a hold of herself, moved to the other side of the island and looked up. Cal's eyes were on her, their blue depths steady, and she was glad she had something in her hands to focus on. Bridgestone wasn't making this easy.

"I can't find Ry."

She frowned and sipped from her mug. "What do you mean you can't find him?"

Cal shrugged. "I haven't seen him since I got back. He hasn't been to the ranch, so I swung by the school, and Mrs. Crabtree told me he hasn't been to class in a few days. She figured he was at the hospital, but Mackenzie says he's been a no-show." His eyebrow rose. "The kid's seventeen. Should I be worried?"

Millie cradled the warm mug between her hands and chose her words carefully. "Ryland's a good kid, but he's had a lot of freedom. Bent's busy running the ranch and he's got Nora to worry about. No one's fault, but Ryland does push the boundaries a bit."

Cal set down his mug and moved closer. "What do you mean by that?"

Millie considered him over the rim of her coffee cup. He was worried, and she figured it was best not to sugarcoat anything. "He got into some trouble a while back. Underage drinking."

"That's not anything we didn't do at that age."

"No, you're right about that, we all did stupid things when we were young, but Ryland stole a car and drove drunk, then ran it into the guardrail out on Dry Creek Road. He's lucky no one was hurt, and real lucky that Sheriff Milson is a family friend. No one knows about it except Bent, the sheriff, and me. I found him on my way to work."

"Shit," Cal muttered. "I had no idea." His eyes darkened. "Why the hell wouldn't Bent tell me that?"

"You don't live here anymore. You're on a different plane of existence. When's the last time you checked in with Bent? When's the last time any of us even crossed your mind? You're not a part of Ry's everyday life." She shrugged. "You're not a part of anyone's life here. Not anymore."

She noted the way his head whipped up. "Those are facts." Millie wasn't entirely sure she'd been able to keep the bitterness from her voice, but she sure hoped so. She was supposed to be over this man.

I am over him.

At least, that's what she needed people to believe.

"Who does he hang out with?" Cal asked after a few moments.

"His buddies are the same ones he's always had. Jake Malone, Frankie Shetts, and Whit Danver. But those boys are diehard jocks. and I doubt they're skipping school. Football is life, and there's a chance they'll make state."

"Ryland isn't on the team?"

"No, he quit last year."

Cal swore under his breath and glanced out the window. "He got a girlfriend?"

"I don't know exactly. The girls have always flitted around him like rabid butterflies, but up until lately, he's never dated anyone exclusive that I know of. He's been by for burgers with Carly Somers a few times, but I don't know if they're serious." She saw Cal's worry and softened her voice. "You might want to swing by the Founder's Cabin. I know he's been spending time up there."

She saw the shock on Cal's face, and she understood it. "Ryland is looking for something, some kind of anchor. His experience with your dad is a lot different from the one you had. Your dad has changed, or at least he's trying."

"He still drinking?" Cal's voice was hard.

"He says he isn't."

Cal didn't reply, and for a moment or two, there was silence. Mr. Higgins jumped onto the counter beside Cal and began to headbutt him, purring so damn loud, it was disgusting.

"Seriously?" She scooped the cat from the counter and put him on the floor. "You know you're not allowed up here." A scowl made its way across her face when the cat immediately leaned into Cal's legs, tail twitching as he meowed loudly.

"Since when do you like cats?" Cal asked, bending down to pet Mr. Higgins's head.

"I don't," she replied, though a small smile tugged at her lips. "Except for this one. He was left behind the Sundowner and I felt sorry for him." Finished with her coffee, she took their mugs and rinsed them in the sink, while Cal shrugged into his coat and pulled on his boots. His hair was long and curled over the collar and she had to blink away an image of her fingers running through the thick waves.

He glanced up just then, and their eyes locked. It was the kind of look that was heavy with memory and things unsaid. And damned if she could look away. A slow heat began in the pit of her stomach, and her breathing hitched.

"You could have called, you know," she said slowly. "Instead of coming out here."

"You wouldn't have picked up."

She opened her mouth, a retort hot on her tongue, but then took a few seconds. He wasn't wrong. "No, I supposed I wouldn't have." She tried to keep things light, because all of a sudden, it felt as if the room was closing in on her. As if the whispers of the past were hiding in the corners. It made her think of stuff she didn't want to think about. "Is that it? Is that all you want?" As soon as the words left her, Millie Sue knew she'd made a mistake.

Cal was silent for a few moments and then spoke quietly, his voice curling around her body like an old friend. "There are a lot of things I want, Mills. Things I shouldn't want. Not anymore. But you know me. I don't play by the rules. I'm back, and it looks like I'll be here for a while, so I'll go slow and ask for one thing at a time." He cracked a half smile as he reached for the door and winked at her. "I'll start with the easy ones."

With that, Cal Bridgestone walked out of her house. She gently closed the door behind him and leaned back, eyes on Mr. Higgins. The cat ran over to the window and stood on his back legs, tail twitching as he looked out the window and meowed. In the space of five minutes, Cal had somehow managed to win over a cat who didn't give a rat's ass about most people unless they had a treat in hand.

It seemed the Bridgestone charm was as potent as ever,

and though she liked to think she was immune, she was only human. A girl with a big old floppy and bruised heart surrounded by flesh and blood. How long before all the bad stuff from the past disappeared and left her longing for more? If Cal stayed in Big Bend for any length of time, she just might be screwed. And damned if she was going to let that happen.

She looked at the cat and scowled. *I need a contingency plan.*

Millie crossed the room and fished out her cell. There was only one person on the planet who truly understood how dangerous Cal was in her orbit.

And he owed her.

CHAPTER 6

LOCATED ON THE OUTSKIRTS OF THE TRIPLE B AND NESTLED among pine and spruce, the Founder's Cabin was barely visible unless you knew where to look. Even though Cal hadn't been to the place in years, he had no trouble finding it. Some things you just don't forget. The small, weathered gray cabin stood in silence, a puff of smoke rising from the chimney like an afterthought, with a small barn off to its right. A beat-up and rusted red Ford, tires covered in chains, was parked there, as well as a sleek black snowmobile.

Up here, the snow wasn't as deep as in the valley, but Cal was glad he'd taken a sled instead of trying to navigate his way with the new truck. With his luck, he'd have gotten stuck for sure. He let the engine idle for a bit and then turned off the machine, sliding off its back to sit on the edge as he took a moment to take in things.

The barn was new and painted to match the cabin, though the trim around the windows was fresh white. It looked like it could hold at least six horses, maybe more. There'd been an attempt to tame the wilderness that surrounded the cabin; some of the trees had been cut back, and burlap-covered bushes of some sort. The porch had been fixed. It used to sag like a son of a bitch. It sported a new railing, while window boxes lay beneath the two windows on either side of the door, and white paint had been added to the frames.

It looked like a picture-perfect cabin in the woods. The kind that brought in big bucks from tourists looking to play cowboy for the weekend, and maybe get in some skiing.

Back in the day, the place hadn't been habitable. There'd been holes in the floors, busted windows, and always a critter or two calling the attic home. That didn't stop him, Mike Paul, and their pals from coming up here all the time. It had been their hangout, a place far away from prying adult eyes and an older brother who'd taken too much of an interest in Cal's shenanigans. It was a place to bring beer and liquor and play songs and get rowdy, maybe grab a kiss from some willing female. He smiled at the memory. Maybe grab more than a kiss. He'd brought Millie up here once. His smile faded at the thought.

God, he was a lifetime away from the kid he'd been, and a part of him missed it. Missed it a hell of a lot.

Cal cleared his throat and shook off the melancholy that had taken hold. There was no point pining for a past long gone. He tugged on his warm wool hat and slowly pulled it off, eyes squinting from the sun as it reflected off the snow. His dad was in there. A man he hadn't seen or talked to in nearly fifteen years. If it wasn't for the fact he was worried as hell about Ryland, he wouldn't be up here at all.

He stared at the door for longer than he should and, before he could talk himself out of it, pushed off from the sled and made his way onto the porch. He held his hand up to knock, but then paused, ashamed that he felt so damn uncomfortable about seeing his old man. About being in a place he'd belonged to so long ago. A place that used to be his.

Fuck it, he thought, and reached for the handle. He didn't give a rat's ass about Manley Bridgestone. The door swung open, and Cal walked inside. He stamped his boots on the rug near the door, his gaze wandering as he tugged off his gloves and shoved them in his coat pocket. The cabin was pretty much one big open room, with a foldaway staircase on the right side that led to what had once been the attic, but had been opened up and was now a loft. It ran the length of the place. He spied a bed and desk up there.

A fire gave the place warmth, flooding it with light and shadow. There was a brown sofa facing it, newer, by the looks of it, with big yellow pillows and a couple of blankets folded neatly across the back. A coffee table with several hardbacks and a few magazines was centered between the sofa, a large pale blue wool rug underneath, and an animal bed lay beside that. The kitchen area was simple with pine cupboards and plain white countertops. There was a decent-sized table off to the side, beneath a large window that showed the mountains out back. Running water was new, and he noted the sink in the kitchen. It was nestled beneath a window, and there was another smaller one by the front door. Between the three of them, enough natural light was able to find its way inside.

Cal turned in a full circle. The place looked homey... lived-in. Hell, there was even a set of floating shelves along the wall near the kitchen that held plants of various shapes and sizes. He had his doubts they were real, but still.

He shoved his hands into the front pockets of his jeans, unsure how to proceed. The house was empty, though with a fire on the go and—he sniffed—chili simmering on the stove, he was betting he'd see his father or Ryland sooner than later. Thinking he should maybe wait outside, he reached for the doorknob, but froze when the back door to the cabin banged open and a large animal, the biggest dog he'd ever seen, bounded inside and immediately headed his way. Cal realized about two seconds before it bared its impressive fangs and growled that it wasn't a dog, but in fact a large gray wolf.

What in the actual hell?

"Penny, stop right there." The wolf gave one last growl and then was silent, its eerie yellow eyes trained on Cal with an intensity he didn't like.

"Penny?" Cal ground out, gaze on the man who now stood a few inches away. He didn't look like the father he remembered. This version of Manley Bridgestone was healthy and fit, with wide shoulders and a sturdy body that was muscled from work. A trim beard couldn't hide the strong jawline, speckled with salt and pepper to match the thick hair atop his head. His eyes were clear and intense, the pale blue of them nearly white in the dim lighting.

Manley Bridgestone was a long way from the withered, bitter drunk Cal had known.

His father didn't look surprised to see him standing in the middle of the cabin, though he didn't say a word. Their gaze held, and then Manley cleared his throat.

"Nora named her," he said, voice deep and rich with that bit of Southern twang he'd inherited from his grandma, one he'd never been able to shake. He nodded at Cal. "Take off your boots. I'm just about to serve lunch."

"You think I'm here for lunch?" Cal asked incredulously.

"I think it's lunchtime and we're about to eat and whatever it is you came to say can wait."

What. The. Fuck.

His father acted as if the past was long gone. As if his

actions and words no longer mattered. As if fifteen years and a whole lotta hurt didn't stand between them. He opened his mouth, a retort hot on his tongue, but his brother walked in from the back, arms laden with chopped wood. He hadn't spied Cal yet and was busy trying to step out of his boots.

The boy has grown.

Cal figured he was nearly as tall as himself, pushing six-four, if he wasn't mistaken. He was filled out enough for a young man his age, long lean lines that still needed some weight. But the bones were there, and if he kept at it, Cal was pretty sure Ryland would be taller than any Bridgestone he knew. Boots successfully off, Ryland glanced up, and damned if it wasn't like looking into a mirror. Eyes the color of cobalt stared back at him, set in a handsome face with high cheekbones, a square jaw, and a generous mouth. A mustache brushed over his upper lip and his hair, while on the long side, was swept back in a carefree manner to curl around the collar of his jacket.

Warmth bloomed in his chest, and Cal cleared his throat, suddenly off-kilter. He felt like an outsider. "Hey, kid," Cal managed quietly.

Ryland nodded, then crossed the room and deposited the wood into a bin by the fireplace. Penny followed him and, once assured that things were good, settled her large body on the bed, though the wolf never took her eyes off Cal.

"What are you doing here?" Ryland asked, darting a look to their father. "Bent's all good, right? Nothing changed?"

Cal found himself nodding. "Yes, he's on the mend."

"So, you're leaving again?" The kid's chin thrust up. Cal sensed some anger, and maybe a little something else. It seemed as if his father wasn't the only one with some bridges to cross.

"Not right away."

"But you'll be leaving."

"Eventually, I guess."

Ryland all but snorted. "We don't need you here, Cal. You don't gotta stay."

More than a little taken aback by his younger brother's attitude, Cal had to take a moment. "I'm here as long as Bent needs me."

Ry didn't bother to hide his eye-roll, though he didn't get a chance to throw another verbal dart at Cal, because their father placed three bowls on the kitchen table. He didn't look at either of them when he spoke.

"We've got plumbing up here now, so both of you wash up. Bathroom's through there." He pointed to a small hall Cal hadn't noticed before. Not bothering to hide his displeasure, Ryland walked past him and disappeared.

Cal stared after his brother, more than a little pissed off himself.

"There's soap in the kitchen too."

Manley had pulled fresh garlic bread from the oven and placed it on the table. He glanced up at Cal. "I don't figure you came all this way to up and leave without your say. You'll get your chance when we're done eating."

"I came here for Ry. I don't have anything to say to you."

"Well, maybe I've got some things to square away, son. Maybe you need to give me the chance to say them."

Surprise, the kind he hadn't felt in years, had his blood burning hot. He didn't get a chance to respond because Ryland appeared and without a word took a seat at the table. Off balance and feeling more than a little out of place, Cal shrugged out of his jacket and hung it on a hook beside the door. He figured his best option was to make nice and break bread with his old man. He'd ease into the school thing with his brother in a way that wouldn't spook the kid. It's what an adult would do.

Cal decided to keep a cool head and play nice. He had no interest in hearing anything his father had to say. He'd seen him clean up, dry out, and then fall back to the bottom of a whiskey bottle more times than he could count. This was a movie he knew well, and the ending was always the same.

He slid his butt onto a chair across from his brother and, in spite of himself, felt his mouth water at the smell of food. He hadn't eaten this morning, so he ladled a generous amount of hot chili into his bowl. Grabbing two slices of garlic toast, he dug in, surprised at how good it was.

Tastes like memory.

He almost said the words aloud as an image of his mother standing over the stove danced in his mind. She'd always made the best chili in the dead of winter. The kind that would stick to bones and fill bellies after a long day of ranching.

He glanced up and caught his dad's eyes on him. He wondered if the old man was thinking the same thing.

The three of them ate in a silence broken only by the occasional snore coming from the mountain of fur that was fully relaxed on the bed by the fireplace. Cal glanced at the wolf—he had questions about the animal.

"Dad found her a couple of years back when she was a pup. The mother was dead, killed by a hunter." Ry glanced at the wolf and smiled. "And all the cubs were dead except Penny."

"Seems like a soft name for such a big animal," Cal replied.

Ryland shrugged. "She's about as soft as a bucking bronco when it comes to strangers. But we're her family.

She'd died defending us." Ry's eyes narrowed, and it was pretty clear who he considered family. For the first time since he'd been back, Cal realized just how big the divide he needed to bridge was. It chased away any more words he had, and with nothing more to say, Cal got up and grabbed the empty plates from the table and rinsed them in the sink.

"I'm gonna check on Indy," Ryland said. He called for Penny, and the wolf followed him outside, leaving Cal alone with his father.

"Indy?" Cal asked casually, turning back to face his father.

"A horse he's been working with. A paint most likely from Pryor that wandered over here in the summer. Ry broke him in last month." There was pride in Manley's voice. "That horse has just about as much stubbornness in him as Ryland. For a while, I wasn't sure which way it was gonna go."

"He's missing school. You okay with that?"

If his father was affected by the coolness of Cal's tone, he didn't show it.

"The boy needed some time."

"I think his teachers would disagree with that."

"You the expert on what goes on in this family?" Manley asked, eyebrows raised.

The fact that Cal was even having this conversation with his father stoked a fire in his chest, one he found hard to contain. "And you are?" He all but scoffed at the notion. "From what I remember, the only thing you're an expert on is whiskey."

"I haven't had a drink in three and a half years." Manley shook his head slowly, those eyes of his never leaving Cal's. "Not one drop." He shrugged. "There ain't a day that goes by

I don't think about it, and some days are harder than others, but I don't let it take me. Not like before."

"Well, good for you, I guess. Forgive me if I don't share your optimism for an alcohol-free future."

"Calvin, I'll always be a drunk, but I'm a sober drunk, and it took a lot to get here. I'm still your father. That affords me some kind of respect."

That mountain inside Cal was crumbling. He nearly shook from the intensity of his feelings. "You lost that right the night Mom died. Don't talk to me about respect."

"I'll never forgive myself for not being there when it happened." His voice rasped. "Never." Manley's face was granite. "There are things I've done. Things I'll never be able to take back or fix. But I'm trying." He sighed and whispered. "I'm trying."

Cal gritted his teeth. "I want Ryland back at the ranch tonight. He needs to get his ass to school in the morning. I'm calling the shots while Bent's in the hospital, and it's something I'm glad for." He paused, sobered at the thought. "I need this. To be back here. I don't think I realized it until just now, but I want you to understand one thing. None of it's for you. I don't want anything to do with you. You can play cowboy or dad or recovering alcoholic, or whatever the hell you want to, because I don't care. I know how that story ends." He slowly exhaled, trying his best to get a hold of his emotions. "I have no idea how you got Benton to agree to you living in the Founder's Cabin, but it won't work with me. I see right through you, old man. You'll have to look for redemption somewhere else."

Manley didn't argue. Instead, he surprised Cal with a question. "How long you here?"

"Why does it matter?"

Manley held his gaze for a good, long while and then slowly shook his head. "I guess it don't."

Cal whirled around and grabbed up his coat. He shoved his feet into his boots and reached for the door.

"Your mom would be proud of what you've done." The words were quiet, but the weight of them was so loud, it nearly took Cal's breath away. He wasn't ready to discuss his mother. Not with Manley.

Chest as tight as his jaw, he said nothing and closed the door behind him. Ten minutes later, he barreled down the mountain, skimming the top of the snow on a sled that could push nearly one hundred and twenty miles an hour. The wind whistled in his ear and the cold stung his face, tugging at his skin and bringing tears to his eyes.

At least, that's what he told himself.

Because damned if he was gonna shed tears for a man who didn't deserve them. He didn't give a crap if his father had changed. It was only a matter of time before it all fell to shit, and Cal had no intention of sticking around to see it happen.

CHAPTER 7

THURSDAY NIGHTS AT THE SUNDOWNER WERE BUSY. RIB-EYE steak with all the fixings was half-price, and for an extra buck, you could get a slice of the best butter cake around. The beer was cold, the crowd was up for anything, and the live music was always a good time. Generally speaking, the place filled up around six in the evening, with the first act hitting the stage by seven. But on this particular Thursday, every single chair at every single table had a butt in it, and the crowd around the bar was four deep before the clock hit four.

"What the hell?" Jennifer, the new server, raised her eyes dramatically at Millie as she grabbed her beer-laden tray. Her bright purple hair was hard to miss, along with the piercings above her left eye, nose, and lip. She was a transplant from New York, had ended up in town the month before when her ailing Honda Civic died on Main Street, and Millie had liked her instantly. Her energy was big, open, and honest. And while it had taken some time (on account of the purple hair and piercings), most of the regulars had warmed up to her as well.

"You couldn't pack any more bodies in here tonight, and we've got hours to go." Jennifer laughed. "You'd think some famous person was in town." She winked. "Seriously, he's just some honkytonk singer, isn't he? I mean, one with a great ass and bedroom eyes, but still."

"I thought you didn't know squat about country singers," Millie replied lightly, not really wanting to engage.

"I don't. But I had to google him. See what the fuss is all about. George is ready to bust his gut, but I get it, he's hot."

Irritated, Millie raised her eyebrow at that. Jennifer was the one person she'd thought would have half a chance of escaping Cal's orbital pull.

"I mean, I even downloaded some of his songs."

You've got to be kidding me.

"He pulls his pants on one leg at a time, same as you."

"I'm guessing most of the women here wouldn't mind helping him in that regard."

"I would," she shot back, a little embarrassed at her reaction. "I mean, he's not..."

"It's okay, Mills. I know all about your history, and on that basis alone, I hate him. I will spit on his boots. In his food. In his beer if you want me to."

"I don't hate him," Millie said softly. "Not anymore."

"Okay, I don't hate him." Jennifer paused, and a look passed between the two women. It was obvious Jenn understood all too well the complications of an ex showing up in town. "I'll still spit on his boot, though."

"Skip the food though," Millie replied with a laugh.

"I'll think about it." With that, Jennifer took her tray and disappeared into the crowd.

Millie grabbed three more jugs from the shelf behind the bar and, as she tapped the new keg and started filling them, kept her head down. Tabitha Bailey and her crew were in the house, and she was doing her best to ignore them. Most nights, it was easy—Millie had had a godly amount of practice—but tonight, she found it hard to do. The women were crowded around the table directly behind Millie, and Tabitha's whiskey-soaked voice saturated the air. It was every man's wet dream, but when Millie heard it, she had to fight the urge to smash her fist into that perfect, surgically refined nose.

The woman had been the bane of Millie's existence since the day she'd arrived in Big Bend nearly two years earlier with her husband, an older man with little to no hair, a pot belly to shade his feet, and about as much personality as a pencil. A developer with an eye to building a fancy ski lodge in the mountains, he quickly realized that he would run out of money long before he saw any profit and had left Big Bend six months in, leaving behind a soon-to-be-divorced Tabitha, along with an undisclosed amount of his money. Word on the street was her prenup had guaranteed at least twenty-five million, and while most folks might have thought she'd stayed in Big Bend because of the scenery and the fancy condo she'd purchased with a million-dollar view to back up the price, Millie knew better.

Tabitha had taken one look at Benton Bridgestone, and, short of taking out a hit on any woman who turned his head, she'd all but claimed the man as her own. She resented Millie's friendship with the Bridgestones and had made it clear just what she thought of Millie Sue, which wasn't much. Millie knew Bent was smart, but he was a man, after all, and when sex was on the table, most of them had a hard time thinking with anything but what was between their legs. Last she'd heard from Mike Paul, Tabitha Bailey was having sleepovers at the ranch and had even had occasion to drop off Nora at school. She got that Benton was lonely, hell, she could relate...but Tabitha Bailey?

"Men are dumb," she muttered as she handed over the last full jug to her cousin.

"I'm not dumb," he replied.

"Do you want me to count the ways?"

Zach made a face and shook his head. "Just because Bridgestone's got you all tied up like a badger in a hole, don't be taking that crap out on me and the rest of my fellow men."

"I don't give a crap about Cal Bridgestone."

Zach snorted. Millie ignored the urge to dump all three jugs over his head. She nodded toward the back of the place. "Take them to table seven."

"I know," he replied with a wink, his handsome face crinkled in a grin. "I put the order in." His grin widened as he backed away, eyebrows raised to the heavens. "See? Not dumb."

Millie couldn't help but smile. She was being a witch and Zach an absolute angel. Not only was he not a server, but he'd been at the bar by seven this morning to look after paperwork and take delivery of their food and liquor order. By the looks of it, Zach probably wouldn't make it home until midnight at the earliest.

"Oh my God, and Mona told me that he took his niece to ballet."

Millie winced at the pitch of Jacklyn's voice and snuck a look at Tabitha's table. Everyone was waiting for Jacklyn to continue. It didn't take a rocket scientist to know they were talking about Cal.

"*And* he stayed for the whole thing." Jacklyn was practically dancing in her boots, her blonde curls bouncing around her face like golden springs. "Mona says he looks real good and he was so nice to everyone, even signing autographs and posing for pictures. Have you met him yet, Tabby?"

Jesus. Millie turned back to the bar and spied Taz Pullman. "Took you long enough," she said lightly.

"I didn't want to seem too eager." He was taller than most, with shoulders a woman could hold on to and the kind of build that came naturally from working outdoors and such. His hair was the color of burnt tobacco, worn long so that the waves went just past his collar, and his features were like a puzzle where all the pieces shouldn't fit, but somehow came together like magic. He was big, dangerously handsome with a quick wit and easy smile. A bull rider who'd won more titles and money than anyone before, he'd left the circuit at the height of his fame when his sister and her husband, a local rancher, had been killed in a car accident, leaving him to raise six-month-old twins on his own. He'd decided to stay in Big Bend and was joined by his mother who'd come from Texas and never left. She lived in town, had bought the old Nelson place, while he took over his sister's ranch. Though some would call it more of a farm. They'd called Big Bend home for the last two years.

"Who's got the kids?" Millie asked with a smile, leaning over the bar.

"Mom." He cracked a grin. "Told her we had a date, and she just about kicked my butt out of the house."

Millie chuckled. Martha Pullman was just shy of five feet. No way in hell she'd be able to kick anyone's ass unless it was a leprechaun.

Taz's smile slowly left his face, and he leaned forward, elbows on the bar. "He here yet?"

"Nope."

"Maybe he'll stay away."

She shook her head. "He's meeting up with Mike Paul."

"I'll take a beer, then, since I've got some time to relax before I get to working on this thing between us."

"There is no thing, champ." Her reply was quick with a teasing tone. "You know this is just for show."

"For now."

Taz held her gaze for a few moments, and Millie shook her head as a slow grin lit up his features. "We did that dance, remember?"

"We did." He took a draw from his longneck.

"And we do good as friends."

"True." He nodded. "But darlin', it would be nice to have some benefits every now and again."

She dropped her gaze. They'd had one hot night together a few years back. Millie had been feeling low, and Taz had been feeling something dark. They'd both been searching for something. Millie was pretty sure she'd just needed to *feel*, and Taz had just needed to forget. They'd kept company plenty of times since then, but had never ended up back in the bedroom.

He was one of her best friends and she his. It was why he'd had no problem agreeing to what she was starting to think was a stupid idea.

She glanced over Taz's shoulder, and like the parting of the Red Sea, folks stood aside as her kryptonite appeared, coming in hot.

She saw the exact moment Cal's eyes landed on Taz, and the look on his face had her gut twisting up hard. Catching on to her discomfort, Taz slowly turned around and leaned his elbows back on the bar.

"This him?" he asked, angling his head close to Millie's. He didn't wait for an answer. "Oh, it's him."

"You don't recognize him from his videos?"

"I don't watch TV, remember?" He chuckled.

Millie realized her error about two seconds too late. If she thought having Taz around would make Cal back off and keep to arm's length, she was mistaken. He headed straight for them, and damn if her heart didn't skip a beat.

Or two.

"Shit," she murmured.

Taz grinned, knocked back the rest of his beer, and winked at her. "This is going to be fun."

Millie didn't have a chance to reply because Cal was in front of her. All six foot four inches of him. He smelled of winter and cold, that crisp clean scent that only seemed to cling to him. His hair was damp, as if he wasn't long out of the shower, the ends frosted from snow. It curled around his neck and touched the collar of his leather jacket. He hadn't bothered to shave, and that square jaw of his was covered in dark stubble, which, of course, only emphasized how beautiful he was. His eyes settled on her with an intensity that was like a jolt of lightning going haywire inside her.

Would this ever stop? This feeling and connection? This deep pit of *something* that sat I her stomach like a stone? What the hell did she have to do to make it end?

"Hey," he said simply holding her gaze a beat longer than she liked.

Taz set down his empty bottle on the bar, effectively breaking the ice. "I'm Taz Pullman. I hear you and Mills are old friends."

Cal's eyebrow shot up at that. "Mills?" His gaze darted to Taz and back to Millie Sue. "She hasn't mentioned you."

And there it was. That slight undertone that got her hackles up.

"No?" Taz's voice was light, and Millie was aware that a lot of eyes were on the three of them. Some folks, those who knew her and Cal's history, were obviously keen to see where they now stood. While others, mostly the female sort, stood like zombies, unable to move as they took in the sight of the two men who, between them, had enough charisma and charm to light up the entire state of Montana.

Taz offered his hand. "Mills and I hang out a lot." Emphasis on *a lot*.

Cal's face gave nothing away. He took Taz's hand and shook it slowly. "Is that so."

"I guess you could say we're together." He flashed a smile at Millie Sue. "Sound about right, darlin'?"

Startled at the direction the conversation was already headed, Millie could only offer a small smile in return and nod.

Cal withdrew his hand and moved toward Millie. "I'll take a draft." His dark eyes never wavered from hers.

"You still like Bud?" she responded, glad she'd gotten rid of the frog in her throat.

"Still like a lot of things." A pause. "Bud being one of them."

"Mike Paul should be here soon." She nodded toward the only unoccupied table in the place. "That's his." She hoped like hell Mike Paul had gotten her text and that he'd back up her bullshit story.

"Nah, I'm good." Cal took the draft from her and leaned against the bar. "Grab one for your buddy here. I'd like to get to know him."

Cal's tone had Millie's Spidey sense on high alert. He wasn't going to make this easy, and she had half a mind to up and leave. But she was in this now. Committed. She took a deep breath, ignored both men, and grabbed another mug from the counter behind her as she glanced up at the clock. Not even seven.

It was going to be a long night.

CHAPTER 8

Cal Bridgestone was having a hard time keeping his shit together. First off, jet lag had settled in something fierce, and the two beers he'd downed since he got to the Sundowner, on an empty stomach no less, didn't help.

It was how things had been shaping up. He'd left the ranch in a bad mood, partially because he was sick of Ryland's attitude, but mostly because he understood it. Ry was right. Cal *had* cut and run and never looked back. He'd used that last argument with his brother as an excuse. Told himself they didn't need him and that they'd all be fine. That Benton would look after things. What did that say about him? He'd all but abandoned his family. In some ways, Cal was no better than his father.

Frowning, he leaned against the bar and listened intently as Pullman chatted to a fan about his former career. The bull rider was some kind of a big deal, and Cal made a mental note to hit up Google and find out just how much of a deal he was.

He wanted to *not* like the guy, but truthfully, he seemed okay. He came across as amiable and easy, and as far as Cal could tell, it was true to life. Other than the fact he seemed to be all up in Millie Sue's business, Cal had nothing bad to say about him.

They'd been cozied up to the bar for almost thirty minutes when Mike Paul appeared.

"Hey," he said, looking from Taz to Cal. "I see you two have met."

"We sure have," Cal replied dryly. "Millie was just telling me all about her bull rider."

"Right." Mike Paul scratched the back of his head. "It's been a long day, and I need to fill the tank. I haven't eaten since ten this morning."

"You hungry?" Cal asked Taz, only because it seemed the polite thing to do. He might think the guy was okay, but that didn't mean he wanted to break bread with him.

"Nah. You guys go ahead. I'm happy to stay here and keep Mills company."

"I'll send Jennifer over to take your order." Millie Sue turned away, and just like that, he was dismissed.

With a curt nod, Cal avoided the pointed stares from the group of ladies to his right and made his way through the bar until he reached the empty table with a Reserved sign in the middle of it.

Mike Paul slid onto the chair across from him, smiled at someone who said hello in passing, and Cal did the same. For a few seconds, Cal worked to rid himself of the tension that had a grip so tight, he felt out of breath.

"What's this Pullman guy's story, and why have you never mentioned him?"

"Not even a hello?" Mike Paul's voice was light. At Cal's raised eyebrow, Mike Paul settled back in his chair. "You never asked."

"Seems like it's something you could have told me."

"Why in hell would I do that? What Mills does and who she does it with is her own business. You gave up any right to keep tabs when you left her behind." Mike Paul's eyes narrowed a bit. "I'm not being an asshole or anything. You did what you felt you had to do back then, but don't put me in the middle of your current shit. Don't ask me to pick sides, because I won't."

Fuck. Cal felt like an idiot because his friend was right.

"I just..." Cal exhaled and slumped in his chair, eyes on the bar as Millie bent over it to speak to Taz. The sight of them so close together wasn't a picture he particularly liked.

"Doesn't Millie Sue deserve to live her life?"

"Of course, she does, but..."

"There are no buts. You can't come back here and pick up where you left off." Mike Paul shrugged. "Besides, she's doing okay from what I can see, so don't screw this up for her."

Their server, a girl with colorful hair and piercings, dropped off a couple of menus. Her smile was wide, but her eyes were cool. At least when they were focused on Cal.

"What will you have, boys?"

"Hey, Jen." Mike Paul was back to his charming self. "I'll have a beer to wash down a couple of pounds of wings."

"Not feeling the rib eye?"

"Not tonight."

"You?" Her eyebrow rose as she waited for Cal to order.

"Same," he replied, watching her walk away before he'd even got the word out of his mouth. "I don't think she likes me."

Mike Paul chuckled. "She's definitely Team Millie."

Cal glanced around at the familiar faces of folks he'd known his whole life. Most of them gave a nod or a small wave and then went about their business. None of them approached his table or acted like he was any different from any other cowboy in the place. They were at the Sundowner to hear music, catch up with friends, and eat some good food. They weren't looking to blow sunshine up his ass, like most of the people in his life—save for Ivy and the band. It was refreshing. Sobering.

And it made him realize a few things.

"I miss this," he admitted softly. "Being here."

"It's a good place for a man to hang his hat," Mike Paul said.

"Yes. It just wasn't for me. Not full-time anyway." He paused. "Millie seems good."

"She is." Mike Paul leaned back in his chair. "She's got her own place now."

"I know. I was there earlier today."

"Oh." Cal could tell Mike Paul was surprised at that. "Then you know she's settled and happy."

"Even has a cat."

"Even has a cat," Mike Paul replied.

"Is she?" Cal asked.

"Is she what."

"Happy?" Cal accepted a beer from Jennifer, who dropped it off and winked at Mike Paul before leaving.

Mike Paul didn't skip a beat. "Yep. She is. Which is why you gotta let her be. In a week or two, or maybe a month, you'll be gone, but Big Bend is Millie's home. She isn't going anywhere."

"She could have." The words were out of his mouth before he realized he'd said them.

Mike Paul shook his head. "She never would have gone with you. Not with..."

"Not with what?" Cal asked, sensing something was off.

Mike Paul was silent for a few seconds and then grabbed

up his beer. "I don't want to relive your relationship with Millie. It's been over for a long time. We all know knocking down that door leads to no good. Let's just be happy we're having a cold beer, eating some of the best wings in the state, and leave it at that."

By the look on his face, Cal knew that Mike Paul was done talking about Millie Sue, and he supposed it was for the best. He decided to change the subject.

"You see Ivy at all?"

"Nope. Didn't know she was back in town."

"Really?"

"Yeah, why?" Mike Paul looked surprised.

"You guys are still in touch. I assumed when we landed, she'd be heading your way at some point."

"Haven't seen her."

"She's being vague about her whereabouts."

"Women can be like that." A pause. "How's Bent?"

"He's doing real good. I stopped in with Nora after I picked her up from ballet."

"Ballet?" Mike Paul snorted. "I would have given my left nut to see you in a room with all those women."

Jennifer dropped off their wings, and when she stepped back, three women stood in her place. Two of them, Cal knew: Jacklyn Davis and Brittany Baker. The tall blonde, however, he'd never laid eyes on. She had a spray tan that didn't quit, shown off nicely by a low-cut red blouse that did nothing to hide a generous rack. Worn jeans that had holes in them, the kind that probably cost a couple hundred bucks, clung to long, lean legs tucked into a pair of brown cowboy boots. Her jewelry was gold, her lips glistened, and a predatory look hung in her eyes.

She was attractive, no doubt about it, but there was a

hardness to her that didn't appeal to Cal, and for some reason, he didn't like the woman on sight.

"Howdy," he said slowly, shifting his gaze to Mike Paul, who was doing his best to ignore the entire thing. "Jacklyn." He nodded. "Brittany. It's been a long time."

"My God, Cal, it's just so good to see you here." Jacklyn beamed holding up her hand, to show off a big diamond. "I'm a Boatright now. Married Jim a few years back. He'll be along in a bit. Just dropping off the kids at his mama's place."

Brittany elbowed her way in front of Jacklyn. "Are you going to sing for us tonight, Cal?"

"I'm not getting on stage," Cal cut in firmly.

"Well, that would be a shame," the tall blonde said, taking a step closer. "Nice to meet you." She held out her hand, the long fingernails as red as her lips. "I'm Tabitha."

Tabitha. Cal blinked. *Tabitha.* Shit, this could not be the woman his brother was—

"Bent and I are close. I'm sure he's mentioned me." Her slow smile widened, her ultra-white teeth a little too bright. She was entirely too comfortable, and though Cal already knew he wasn't a fan, he wasn't in the habit of being rude to a lady.

"Bent was kinda out of it when I saw him last," Cal replied. "But Nora has."

"Isn't she just the sweetest thing?" The woman's smile held firmly in place. "I swear she's like my own little girl."

"Spitting image of Daisy Mae," Jacklyn said, nodding. Whatever else the woman was going to say was cut short by the side-eye Tabitha shot at her.

"I wouldn't know," Tabitha said lightly, gaze lingering on the men. "So, gentlemen, mind if we join? I'd like to get to know Bent's brother a little better."

Mike Paul nearly choked on a wing.

Cal reached for one. "Mike Paul and I got some catching up to do, but maybe another time." Tabitha didn't hide her surprise all that well, and Cal got the feeling she wasn't used to rejection.

"I was thinking of stopping by the ranch tomorrow," she said slowly.

"Yeah?"

"To visit with Nora. She's such a sweet little thing."

"That so?"

"After I stop in to see Bent, that is."

"I believe it's just family allowed at the moment." He turned so there was no mistaking his meaning. "It's probably for the best that we keep things fairly quiet with Benton and Nora."

"For the moment," she said carefully.

He nodded. "For the moment."

She smiled, though it didn't warm her ice-blue eyes a bit. "Promise me you'll let me know when I can get in to see Bent."

"I'll do my best."

"Mike Paul knows where I live." She waited a few moments. "It was nice meeting you, Cal. I look forward to seeing you soon." She turned and left them, with Jacklyn and Brittany uttering quick goodbyes before following suit.

He glanced over to Mike Paul, more than a little confused. "That's the woman Bent's been hooking up with?"

"Something wrong with your eyes? She's hot." His reply was matter-of-fact.

"And trouble."

Mike Paul shrugged and reached for another wing. "There's been no one serious since Daisy Mae. Benton's no different from any other guy. He needed someone to scratch an itch. The kind that don't go away unless it's scratched right. She just happened to come along and," Mike Paul grinned slyly, "her nails are sharp, if you get my meaning. Or so I've heard."

Cal swiped at the corner of his mouth and grabbed up his beer. "Too sharp. If Bent's not careful, she'll leave him with scars. The kind that hurt."

"Kind of like the ones you left on Millie." The words were quiet, but man, did they dig deep.

Cal eased a sigh and slumped into his chair. "Yeah," he replied slowly, appetite long gone. "Just like those ones."

CHAPTER 9

TIME PASSED QUICKLY FOR MILLIE SUE. THE BAR WAS PACKED, people were drinking and eating and spending their cash, and she was nearly run off her feet trying to keep up. It was a good thing, keeping busy. Helped her focus and keep her eyes off the table tucked away in the back. Millie was too busy filling orders and running food to care that Tabitha had made a beeline toward Cal, or that Brandy Davidson had found her way over, as well as Judith McLaren and Angel Saunders. Good God, even Mary Margaret had sashayed over. Bad enough that Tabitha was clearly trying to get her claws into him, but it was Angel she had a problem with.

Angel had been the one he'd—

"Hey, you need to get up there."

What?

Millie whipped her head up, a half-filled jug of beer in hand, and raised her eyebrow at Taz. With a frown, she shook her head, though she became aware everyone was staring at her.

"Come on, Mills. It's tradition."

The voice came from the stage, and she glanced over, a sinking feeling in her stomach when she spied Dave Travis, the best picker in the county and a staple on Thursday nights. His band was a local favorite, and Millie aways hopped on stage for a couple of songs.

Panic.

Cold and hot at the same time made her stomach turn. She tried to smile, holding up the jug she was filling. But before she had a chance to say no, her cousin grabbed it and gently pushed her.

He leaned close and whispered. "You gotta get up there, Millie. He's looking over here, and you don't want him to think you're afraid."

"I'm not," she sputtered, "I..." But the shit going on inside her belly told another tale. Millie inhaled slowly and tried to smile as folks began to cheer. She didn't have to look toward the back to know Cal's eyes were on her. She felt them. Burning laser beams that watched too closely. Was he thinking about the last time she'd been on stage? *With him?*

"Screw him," Taz said, moving closer. "You got this. Sing for me or for John Deere-hat guy who just got rejected by the hot blonde in the tight jeans. Or his buddy who slipped the blonde his number when hat guy wasn't looking. That's going to be a problem later, don't you think?" He winked. "You got this."

She held his gaze for a heartbeat and nodded. Okay. She could do this. But she wasn't singing for anyone but herself.

Millie jogged through the crowd, a fake smile pasted to her face, and took the guitar Dave offered her. She strummed a few chords, tweaked the low E, strummed a few more chords, and then began to play. It was like waking memory, being on stage, playing this instrument and singing from her heart. The stage lights shone in her eyes, which made the crowd nothing more than a dark jumble of shadows that moved to the music she was creating. It made it easy for her to block everything out. To block *him* out.

And just sing.

Millie and Dave Travis ran through several songs, staples by Cash, Waylon, and Cline. Eventually, the music did what it always managed to do. It soothed the rough edges, made all the broken pieces inside her fit, and she felt light and free. Head down, she picked a rambunctious song that had the crowd cheering and stomping their feet, her rich voice cajoling the kind of notes not many could reach. She didn't showboat. She wasn't that kind of singer—she was a master of melody, of highs and lows and all the in-betweens that melted together in a tapestry of song that made most folks stop dead and listen, while the others moved and swayed and lost themselves in her voice.

Millie played another song. And then another, her face turned to the light, eyes closed as the music swelled and then softened until it was just her and the guitar and a haunting melody that had the bar watching in silence. It wasn't one of hers, but a Hank Williams song that transcended time and place. It was full of longing and sadness, and as she opened up her heart and let the music take her, Millie got lost in it.

So lost she didn't realize at first that another voice had joined hers. Or that the energy had changed. It had thickened and widened, gotten bigger than just her. His voice wrapped itself around hers, as if his harmony wasn't meant for anyone other than Millie, and it felt like *home*.

When they finished the song, she kept going, caught up

and unaware, and Cal followed along, his voice a perfect foil to hers. When she finally stopped the place was utterly bereft of sound. Like a vacuum had sucked it all out. But then a clap echoed, and another...and another, until the entire bar erupted.

Millie slowly opened her eyes and gave a small nod. Her throat was full, and she wouldn't have been able to talk if she wanted to. She handed Dave the guitar and walked off stage into the shadows to the right. Her heart was nearly beating out of her chest, her body shaking from adrenaline, when she felt a hand on her elbow. She counted to ten and turned around. Cal stood, his eyes hooded as he watched her.

"That was—"

"Don't," she interrupted him, hand up.

He paid no mind. "I've never heard anyone sing like you," Cal said, voice low and intimate. "I miss it." He took a step closer. "I miss you, Mills." His voice wavered. "I miss all of it."

Millie gazed up at this man who, at one time, had meant everything to her. A man she'd dreamt of a life with. A man she'd given all of herself to, only for him to leave her on a cold night in February while the snow fell and the silence pressed in.

He'd broken her. He'd crushed her spirit and dreams and didn't even know it. Or if he did, he sure as hell didn't care.

Her gaze fell from his as a burn began to build in her gut. It spread like wildfire as memories and pain and longing and anger jumbled together, making her feel sick.

He *missed* her?

"Don't ever do that again," she said through clenched teeth.

Cal's mouth tightened at her tone. "Do what?" he asked carefully.

"You know the rules in this place." Her chin jutted forward. "You don't take the stage until you're asked. It's not a free-for-all. Especially for out-of-towners."

Cal's mouth fell open, and for the first time in the last few days, Millie felt like she had a modicum of control.

"You're not one of us anymore. We don't care that you're some fancy singer from Nashville who wears five-hundred-dollar boots and rides around on a plane with balls on the side of it."

"Balls?"

"The bull on the side of your plane?" Was that a smile touching his mouth? Millie Sue Jenkins was so mad, it was a miracle smoke wasn't coming out her nose and ears.

"Pretty sure Dirk's privates aren't on display." That *was* a smile.

"Dirk?" she all but spat at him.

"It's what we call the bull. He's the logo for my label." That smile she wanted to punch widened. "And just so you know, my boots cost me twelve-fifty. That's one thousand two hundred and—"

"Yeah, I get it. Only an asshole would spend that much on a pair of boots that are no different from the ones for sale at the Co-Op."

"They're Italian."

"I don't care."

"Why are we fighting about my boots and Dirk?"

"That's not what we're fighting about," she retorted. "Actually, we're not fighting. I'm telling you that I don't want to share a stage with you ever again. My place, my rules."

"I think you're afraid," he said so softly, she barely heard him.

"Are you high?" she said, anger making her voice sharp.

Her stomach flipped over because suddenly, he was so close to her she could count his damn eyelashes. See the freckle near his right eye. Smell that scent that shouldn't smell so damn good. Not when she was furious and pissed and...

"Admit it, Millie Sue. We just created magic up there."

"Magic."

He nodded, watching her closely.

"There's a problem with our kind of magic, Cal. It only lasts as long as the stage lights are on us." She stepped away. "I'm not doing this with you."

"You guys need to get a room or find your way to a boxing ring. Seriously. It feels like I've walked back in time."

Chest heaving, Millie Sue tore her eyes from Cal. Standing a few inches away was a woman. Her cheeks were red from the cold. Snow clung to dark lashes, which in turn framed a pair of Bridgestone blue eyes that seemed luminescent. Hair the color of rust spilled over her shoulders, the waves anchored beneath a thick blue wool hat, as she stamped excess snow from her boot-covered feet. At five foot three inches, she was the smallest of the Bridgestones, though her stature did nothing to diminish her personality. She was a firecracker, a blinding ray of energy, and someone Millie loved with all her heart. It had been too long.

"Scarlett," Cal said softly.

"Hey, big brother."

"You're back," Millie said, unable to hide her smile.

"I am. I came as soon as I heard about Bent, but I was in Florence and there was a problem with the train and booking tickets and..." Her voice trailed off with a shrug. "It took longer than I expected."

"Benton will be so happy to see you. I hope you're staying longer than last time?"

Scarlett opened her mouth to reply, but Cal's shocked voice stopped her cold.

"You're pregnant."

Millie's gaze dropped, and for the first time, she noticed an unmistakable baby bump.

"Sure can't get nothing past you," Scarlett replied, chin thrust forward. "Europe was a hoot." There was a thickness to her voice, a slight tremble to her chin. "I brought a little of it back with me."

For a few seconds, no one said anything, and then Cal stepped forward. He enveloped his little sister in his arms, and as Scarlett began to cry, Millie moved away. The two of them needed time to themselves. There was a lot for the Bridgestones to process.

And as for her and Cal? Something had just shifted between them. It was big and emotional and hard. But what did it mean? Was he firmly in her past, or tangled up in an uncertain future?

Future? Where the hell had that thought come from? Was she crazy? There was no future here.

She glanced back at the two of them, her heart squeezing as she watched Cal cradle his sister like she was breakable. No one could ever question his love for his family. He just had a hard time showing up for them.

Cal glanced over to her just then, his expression shuttered, eyes unreadable. She held his gaze until he turned away and headed for the exit, his sister at his side.

Millie swore under her breath and tossed her rag in frustration.

"You okay?" Taz sidled up beside her. "That looked intense."

"I don't know," she said softly. "He drives me crazy. Just when I think I can deal with him, with all of him, with all of us, or at least what used to be us, the world tilts and the ground shifts and I don't know what any of it means."

"You don't need to figure it out tonight." When she said nothing, Taz pushed away from the bar and gave her a hug. "You know where I am if you need anything." He kissed the top of her head and disappeared into the night.

Mike Paul slid his arm across her shoulders. "Never thought I'd see you two on stage together again."

"I guess hell froze over." Her words were light, but her friend knew the weight behind them.

"I know this probably isn't what you want to hear, but damn, you guys sounded great." He paused as she stepped out of his embrace. "I think he's changed, Mills, but I don't know if he's changed enough. You need to be careful."

"Don't worry about me. I know how this ends. Cal will be here until his brother is released from the hospital. He'll dive back into our lives because a part of him truly feels bad for leaving like he did. For not checking in. But when he needs to get back on the road, when he needs to hear those thousands of fans screaming his name and lifting him up with whatever superpower they have, he'll be gone, probably in the middle of the night when he doesn't have to face any of us. He needs to be away from here to forget about everything that would make him stay."

Mike Paul didn't answer because he probably knew Millie Sue was right. He tipped his head and left.

Outside, the snow had stopped falling, a blanket of white that glistened like diamonds underneath a November moon. Millie locked up and five minutes later was heading down the road, her headlights the only things to cut through the darkness.

She decided not to think about Cal or any of it. She would go home, snuggle with Mr. Higgins, and pretend that her world hadn't just changed.

If anything, Millie Sue Jenkins was sure good at pretending.

CHAPTER 10

Less than a week ago, Cal had been on stage with the band, performing his first of three sold-out dates in Sydney. It had been a triumphant return to the land down under with critics calling his show a once-in-a-lifetime event. His popularity had soared with the release of his previous album, and the new one had sent him into the stratosphere. He was on par with Garth or Swift.

He was grateful. He knew the odds each artist faced when trying to break out in a saturated market were huge. But his work ethic was strong, and as he began to gain traction, he gave as much as he got. And then some. Now, with several albums under his belt, his tour was an event, and Cal played for well over three hours each time he hit the stage. He had the crowd singing along to every song until the final note. And even then, they stayed, hoping for more.

It was a life most folks couldn't imagine, and one he had a love/hate relationship with. As much as he loved being onstage, feeding off that energy, sometimes when the lights were gone, when his band was holed up in their suites and he was on his own in the dark, he asked himself, when did it get so big?

When did it become this machine?

If Bent hadn't been in that accident, he'd be somewhere in Europe. Hell, he didn't pay attention to the details. When Cal was on tour, time melted into moments strung together by highs and lows. He relied on Ivy to get him where he needed to be. But it never failed to amaze him how quickly life could turn. And Lord knows, he'd been hit with that particular hammer more than once. As it was, instead of staring at the faceless crowd of eighty or so thousand souls, singing his heart out and inhaling enough of that energy to get him through the next show, he'd been sitting in the dark for hours, listening to the wind moan and rumble against the windowpanes.

It was the second night of nearly no sleep, and he needed caffeine.

With a groan, he stretched, rolling his shoulders to get the knots out. Outside, it was getting lighter, which meant he had maybe an hour or so before Nora came running down the stairs as if a pack of wolves were chasing her. Who needed a crowd of eighty thousand? He could borrow some of his niece's energy and be fine.

He slid out of the leather chair that was tucked into the corner of his brother's office and, running his hands through his hair, made his way down to the kitchen. He was going to have to start sleeping in a bed, or his back would be giving him problems.

Cal found the coffee grinds and made a pot the old-fashioned way—none of those throwaway pods in this Bridgestone house. He'd just poured himself a strong one when a sound caught his attention. He spied Scarlett rummaging through the fridge, the top of her head barely visible over the door. She came up for air, a large orange juice container in one hand, a fist of grapes in the other. After pouring a big glass, she climbed onto one of the tall chairs at the counter and immediately shoved several grapes into her mouth. Her hair was a tangled mess secured to the top of her head with a bright pink fuzzy tie, and she wore a green T-shirt with a pink unicorn across her chest and a matching pair of shorts. The top was two sizes too small, and her swollen belly was visible.

"Sorry, I don't have any clothes that fit."

Shit. He'd been caught staring. "You don't have to be sorry." His reply was light.

"You haven't slept yet," she said, taking a gulp of juice.

"Why do you say that?"

"Because you look like shit." Scarlett cracked a smile. "You're not twenty-two anymore, Cal. A man your age needs his rest."

"Shut up."

She laughed at that, though her smile slowly faded, and she sighed. On the ride out to the ranch, she'd told him about the man she'd met in Ireland. A man she'd given her heart to. A man who'd smashed it to pieces. And who, after she told him she was pregnant, had accused her of sleeping around and said it wasn't his. Then he'd dropped the bomb that he was already married. That his wife thought he was traveling for work.

"For four months?" she'd asked him incredulously.

He'd just shrugged and not bothered to answer. They'd been staying at a pub outside of Dublin, and when she woke up in the morning, he was gone, along with all the cash she'd had. His cell number no longer worked. He'd all but disappeared into thin air.

"It's weird," Scarlett said softly. "Being here without Bent and Dad and..." She looked down at her hands.

"Without Mom," Cal replied.

She sat back on the chair. "Have you seen him?"

Cal didn't have to ask to know who she was talking about. He nodded.

"He's not drinking anymore. At least he wasn't when I was here last."

"So I hear."

Scarlett pushed her empty glass with her fingers. "Bent's going to need help. You know that, right? He can't run this place if he's not at one hundred percent, even with Dallas. Lord knows he's got his hands full as it is. And I—" She looked down at her belly. "I don't know what I can do to help."

He heard the fear in her voice and reached for her hand. "I'm here now, and I'm not going anywhere until this family is back to where it needs to be."

"Heard that before."

They both turned as Ryland walked into the kitchen, chest bare, blue plaid sleep pants barely hanging on to slim hips. His thick hair was all over the place and sleep still clung to his eyes as he scratched at the peach fuzz on his chin.

"You're still pregnant," he said to his sister as he poured himself a glass of juice and then topped up hers.

"You're still annoying."

Ry cracked a smile. "Some things never change."

"I'm hungry." Nora ran to Cal and tugged on his hand. "Can I have pancakes with smiley faces on them?" She twirled and giggled. "Pretty please?" She paused when she spied Scarlett. The little girl had been asleep when Cal had brought his sister home the night before. "Auntie Scar! You got a beach ball in your belly."

"She's got more than that," Ryland said under his breath, ducking a swat from his sister as he made his way to the cupboard. He grabbed the pancake mix from the cupboard, while Cal got the eggs and milk out of the fridge, along with peameal bacon and bread. The two of them worked together to prepare the food while Nora kept Scarlett entertained with her endless questions and shrieks of joy when she found out a baby, and not a beach ball, was inside her Auntie's belly.

"Is it a boy?" Nora asked, waiting patiently for Ryland to draw a chocolate syrup smiley face on her pancake.

"I don't know." Scarlett's voice was light, and Cal knew his sister was doing a good job hiding her pain.

"Well, when will you know?" Nora's eyes were wide as she listened.

"When it's born."

"And when is that gonna be? Tomorrow?"

Scarlett laughed. "No, sweetie. Around the New Year." Her eyes met Cal's. It seemed his sister was farther along than he'd thought.

They ate their food, and, once finished, Ryland offered to take Nora to school.

"That mean you going to class?" Cal asked before heading up to shower.

"Yeah. I guess."

"Good. Thanks for taking Nora. Do you need me to pick her up or—"

"No. I got it." His brother paused. "You going to see Bent?"

"Yeah. I'll take Scarlett this morning."

"When can I see Daddy?" Nora's eyes were wide as she gazed up at Cal.

"I'll ask the doctor today. I'm hoping soon."

"Can you give him a big squishy hug and a kiss on his nose?"

"I can." Cal patted his niece on the back. "You need to get on upstairs and get dressed." He winked. "And no cowboy boots today, got it?"

He waited until Ryland and Nora disappeared before he blew out a ragged breath. He hadn't realized how tight he'd been holding himself until that moment.

"I can't remember being that young," Scarlet said. "Not knowing about the bad stuff."

"Not all kids are that lucky," Cal replied.

"No. I suppose they're not." She paused. "I had tickets to your show at Wembley. It was supposed to be next week. Ivy sent them months ago." She gave him a hug and murmured against his chest. "It must be hard to give all that up and come back here."

"Not as hard as I thought it would be." The admission surprised him, and he had to clear his tight throat before he could continue. "I'm sorry I've been out of the loop. That I haven't checked in."

"You've been too busy being a superstar."

"It's no excuse."

"No," she replied softly. "It's not. But you're here now." She paused. "Was it hard to see Millie Sue? We didn't talk about her last night."

Ignoring her question, Cal kissed the top of his sister's head. "Go on and shower. We'll head to town when you're ready and see Benton. You'll be good for him."

"Will I?" she asked softly. "I think I'm going to be one more problem. One more thing for him to worry about."

"That's what families do, isn't it? Worry about each other?"

Scarlett's smile was small as she backed away. "We used to. Once."

She disappeared and left Cal alone with the mess of dishes. Some things never change. By the time he'd cleaned up the kitchen, Nora had skipped by, grabbed her lunchbox, then followed Ryland out into the crisp November morning. The snow was here to stay, which wasn't all that unusual for this part of the country, and with a start, Cal realized that Thanksgiving wasn't far away.

When the hell had that snuck up on him? He searched his pockets for his phone, thinking he'd left it in the office, when he heard the front door open and slam shut from the wind. He'd barely taken two steps into the hallway when Ivy Wilkens appeared, glasses frosted, her hair a wild mess from the wind.

"Where's your phone?" she asked, glaring at him through her fogged-up lenses.

"Good morning to you too."

"Is it?" She walked past him and didn't stop until she had a cup of coffee in hand. She took a sip and leaned back against the counter. "Have you looked at your phone this morning?"

"No." Cal frowned. "Where the hell have you been anyway? You just disappeared."

"I had some things to do."

"Like what?"

"Seriously?" Ivy's eyebrow rose dramatically.

"Mike Paul was wondering where you were."

"Let him wonder. If he wants to know where I am, he can call."

"Someone pour shit in your cornflakes?" Cal asked with a frown.

"Actually, I haven't had anything to eat yet." She walked over to the cupboard and pulled out a yellow box with a bear on the side of it. "I suggest you go and get your phone so we can have a conversation about the shitstorm you created, because it's going to get interesting around here and not everyone is going to like it."

"What the hell does that mean?"

Ivy shook her head and shoved dry cereal into her mouth. "Find your phone," she managed to mumble. "Then we'll talk."

The girl was exaggerating. What kind of trouble could he have gotten himself into? Heck, he'd only been back in town two days. Cal left Ivy in the kitchen and trotted back to the office. He found his cell on the floor by the chair. He touched the screen and paused—there were one hundred and sixteen new text messages waiting for him. He started to scroll. And then he scrolled some more. By the time he returned to the kitchen, he'd scrolled through most of them. He looked across the room at Ivy.

"I told you to stay away from Millie Sue. Didn't I say that at least ten thousand times on the flight from Sydney?"

"It's not that bad," he said slowly, gazing down at the TikTok he'd been sent. It was one of a dozen or so.

"Not bad? She's going to kill you. She's all over every single social media platform there is. How could you not know that jumping on stage with her was not going to get posted online? I've been fielding calls all morning. Everyone wants to know who she is. They want to know where you've been hiding her. They want to know if she's your *girlfriend*."

"She sounds amazing."

"Yeah. She does." Ivy shook her head in disgust. "I wouldn't want to be you right now."

"Come on, really?" he stared across the kitchen at Ivy.

"*Really*," Scarlett said, walking into the kitchen. She glanced at Ivy. "Men are dumb."

"You're not going to get an argument from me," Ivy retorted.

"Whatever," he muttered under his breath. "We're adults. We're not kids anymore. Millie and I are fine."

"If you say so." Ivy didn't look convinced. "Your publicist is waiting on an answer. You might want to get on that."

He looked from Ivy to Scarlett. What the hell was wrong with these women? They were overreacting. Had to be. Shaking his head, Cal left them to head up to his bedroom. He needed a long hot shower. More than that, he needed time to figure out how to deal with Millie Sue. Because as much as he hated to admit it, Ivy wasn't wrong.

Millie Sue Jenkins splashed all over social media, trending on more than one platform, wasn't a good thing. Especially with him at her side.

She was going to be pissed. The only question, was... how bad was it gonna be?

CHAPTER 11

It was five thirty and already dark when Millie made it back to town.

She'd spent the better part of the day holed up at her place, eating leftover pizza and watching *Friends* reruns with Mr. Higgins. A part of her would have liked to have stayed put, but she'd promised Bent she'd stop in to see him. She knew that Cal and Scarlett had already been to the hospital with Nora, so her chances of running into the only man in Big Bend she wanted to avoid were pretty low. That was courtesy of Mike Paul. He'd sent her a text message an hour earlier. Thank God for buddies looking out for her.

She wasn't ready for that particular Bridgestone just yet.

She didn't want to think about the night before. Of Cal being onstage with her again. Of opening herself up and exposing her weakness for the world to see. How the hell had she let that happen? She'd all but curled up into a ball when she'd first opened her phone, which had blown up with so many messages, it took her forever to scroll through them. They all had one common denominator: a link to Insta or something like it. Her cook, George Caplan, had sent one link along with at least thirty emojis, followed by a big old red heart.

Her heart had sunk, and after mulling it over, she'd finally clicked on the link.

In the clip, she was on stage singing a tune she'd written years ago, a melancholy song of love, loss and longing, and Cal was up there beside her, his harmony a perfect blend to her voice, something that hadn't changed.

Why she'd started strumming that song was beyond her. She'd literally forgotten he was up there with her. It happened when she was on stage. The world fell away, the music moved through her, and she laid bare everything inside, comfortable in her little Sundowner cocoon and the community of Big Bend.

Except this time, the world had peeked in. An outsider, none other than Tabitha, had taken the video and posted it online. It had been a self-serving post, a way to look as if she was "in the know." She might have not meant for it to gain as much traction as it had, but it was out there. As of now, Tabitha's post was homing in on one million views and had gone viral, shared many times over.

Millie knew this because, despite herself, she'd looked at it more than once.

"Shit," she said roughly as she pulled into the parking lot of the hospital. She'd worked so hard to build a life without him. And she'd been fine. She'd moved on. She was happy. Kind of. And now her little corner of the world was in peril. Her life could unravel at any moment, and her secrets, the ones she'd tucked away in a place she never visited, might come to light.

If that happened?

"Stop it," she murmured, hopping out of her truck. As

her grandma used to say, *no sense in borrowing tomorrow's trouble.*

Snow crunched underfoot, and she yanked up the collar of her coat. The air was crisp, the night sky a brilliant wash of stars as she entered the hospital and headed to the third floor. She kept her head down as she walked down the corridor, but she was aware that folks were staring. By the time she made it to Bent's room, her jaw was tight, and she had to work to unclench her teeth.

Mackenzie was sitting on the end of Bent's bed, chuckling at something he'd just said, when she walked inside. They both looked her way, and Mackenzie got to her feet, eyes warm as she smiled at Millie.

"We were just talking about you," she said with a wink. She turned back to Bent. "This is your last visitor. Even though you're on the road back, you still need to rest. Especially if you want to be home for Thanksgiving."

Mackenzie grabbed her tablet. "Don't be too long," she whispered as she passed by.

Millie walked to the bed and kissed Benton on the cheek. "I'm so glad to see you're on the mend."

"Takes more than a bump on the head to keep this boy down." His voice was low, he spoke slowly, and it was obvious he was tired.

"Can I get you anything?"

"No," Bent said. "They're looking after me like I'm something special."

"That's what we call the Bridgestone effect," Millie replied with a chuckle.

"More like the Cal effect. Those nurses are buzzing around something fierce, hoping he'll make a second visit."

Her smile slowly faded, and she glanced away. "I'm sure he factors into it."

"Who knew a coyote running into the road would bring our Cal home." He paused, those knowing eyes settled on her. "I know it can't be easy for you."

"I'm good," she replied. "We're good."

"I saw the video."

"They allow phones and devices in here with all this equipment?" she asked lightly.

"It's me, Mills. You can talk to me."

"I don't hate him anymore, if that's what you're wondering."

"I don't think you ever did," he said quietly.

"No, I suppose you're right on that count." She flashed a half-hearted smile. "I guess I don't resent the air he breathes. I know we're never going to be together. His choices are always going to be different from mine, so I'm over it. I'm over *him*. He's just a guy from my past."

Silence followed her declaration, and Bent took a moment, as if he were trying to decide the right thing to say. "I saw the video. You don't have to pretend with me."

God. This man saw everything. How many others had? Chest tight, she attempted a smile. "But I do pretend when I have to," she said. "It's how I cope."

"Have you ever thought about telling him? Maybe it'll make it easier to unburden yourself. Make it easier to pretend." Bent's kind eyes nearly brought her to tears. "I think he's still in love with you, and I know you're—"

"There's no point, Benton," she interrupted before he said out loud the one thing she couldn't admit to herself. "He's leaving as soon as you're back on track, and I can't see a way for us to ever be together and be happy."

She saw the confirmation on his face. Everyone knew Cal would leave Big Bend as soon as he could.

"Funny how life is." Bent heaved a sigh and lay back on

his pillow. "Daisy's been gone four years, and there's not a day that goes by I don't think of her. As much as she drove me crazy to the point I didn't know which way was up or down. As much as she did spiteful awful things. She wasn't good for no one, not even her own daughter. But that doesn't mean I don't wonder where she is and what she's doing with who. We weren't good for each other, but it doesn't make it any easier. We don't always fall for the right person. The lucky ones do."

Millie Sue pressed a kiss to his cheek. They'd always had this bond, this linked sadness. "Maybe one day, we'll be lucky," she whispered.

"Maybe."

"Sounds like you'll be home for Thanksgiving?" She changed the subject because she'd had enough of the past.

"That's the plan. You've seen Scarlett." It wasn't a question.

"Yes."

"Another baby, and she didn't say much about the father."

"I'm sure you'll get the story sooner rather than later."

"We're a sad bunch, aren't we?"

"What do you mean?"

Benton shrugged. "Us Bridgestones. We can't seem to find any kind of happiness. It's as if when Mom died, all of it got sucked away with her. Dad spiraled, and though he's stopped drinking, that's no guarantee he won't fall off the wagon." He paused, as if gathering some more strength. "Even though I was as high as a kite when Vivian was here, something's up with her. I don't think it's anything good. With her it never is. Hell, she couldn't wait to get out of Big Bend."

"Families are complicated."

"No shit." Bent grimaced. "Do you think people can change?"

Millie considered her answer. "I think we're all hard-wired to be a certain way, and sometimes even if we want to change, we can't."

"Well, that's not what I wanted to hear."

A lump formed in her throat, and she knew Bent was thinking about little Nora. His and Daisy's past made hers and Cal's look like a walk in the park by comparison. The door to his room opened, and a nurse entered. She looked at Millie.

"Sorry, but I'm going to have to ask you to leave. I need to check on a few things."

"Shoot, Cara, can't it wait?" Benton's charm was palpable, and the nurse, an older lady with tidy, dyed red hair and a petite build, blushed, her cheeks nearly as dark as her hair.

"Don't you try that on me, sir," she said with a wink. "I know what you're all about, Benton Bridgestone."

"You sure do," he replied with a slight grin. "I think in the last few days, you've seen pretty much all of me."

"My word, but you're a devil."

Millie laughed and said her goodbyes with a promise to return. She had no doubt Bent would be home for the holidays. The man was too damn stubborn not to be.

She was a few feet from the nurse's station when she spied Tabitha Bailey in a heated conversation with Mackenzie Fischer.

"But everyone knows that Bent and I are together." Tabitha's voice rose as she squared off with the doctor. Dressed head to toe in black, her hair looked like platinum sunshine spilling down her shoulders.

"I'm sorry, but it's only family allowed. Mr. Bridgestone is recovering from serious injuries, as you know."

"*Unbelievable.*" Her voice spat venom. "Does Bent know I've been coming by?"

"He's aware."

Tabitha glanced up just then and spied Millie Sue. Her chin jutted forward, and her eyes were glacial. "Since when is Millie Sue Jenkins family?"

Mackenzie all but rolled her eyes as she stepped back. "Around these parts, the Jenkinses and the Bridgestones *are* family."

"Well, if he's okay to see *her*, I think it's ridiculous you won't allow me five minutes."

Millie couldn't hear Mackenzie's reply, but the doctor headed toward the elevators and disappeared from view. With no choice but to walk past Tabitha, Millie moved toward the exit as well, but was stopped by the clearly agitated blonde.

"Can you believe this?" she said. "Since when is a hospital run like a police state?"

"They have rules for a reason, Tabitha. I only spent a few minutes with Bent, and it's obvious he needs to rest. We want him home by the holidays."

Her eyebrow shot up at that. "He's going to be home for Thanksgiving?"

Millie could all but see the wheels turning in the woman's head. Tabitha's lips pursed as she dug out her cell phone. "I guess I'll send him a message."

She didn't bother to let Tabitha know that Bent's phone had been destroyed in the accident and he didn't yet have a replacement. She made to walk by her, but Tabitha had a parting shot.

"So, you and Cal. I didn't know you two had history."

Millie's hackles were up in an instant, and she didn't bother to keep the dislike from her voice. "Why would you? We were kids, and it was over a long time ago."

Tabitha's eyes narrowed. "It didn't look over last night."

"That's your interpretation."

"It is." Tabitha smiled, a cold sort of thing that added zero warmth to her eyes. "And it's funny how everyone clams up when I ask about you two."

"We like to keep our private stuff private."

"Please, small-town gossip is a rite of passage for places like this."

"But you're an outsider, Tabitha. One with an agenda. That's the difference." Gone were the niceties. Millie didn't care anymore.

"Huh." Tabitha slowly slipped her cell phone back into her purse. "Angel Marino doesn't play by your stupid rules. She went on and on about you two."

"Angel likes to talk. She always has."

"You're right about that." Her voice was deceptively warm. "I know she was the one spreading all that unfortunate gossip about me and my ex when we split. And just for the record, I dumped him. It wasn't the other way around."

"Noted." It was hard to keep the sarcasm out of her voice. Especially when she knew for a fact her ex had cut his losses, of which Tabitha was the biggest, and then he'd run.

"I've got a question, though." Tabitha Bailey was a predator, and right now she had Millie Sue in her sights. "I find that when people protest too much, it's usually for a reason." Gone was the fake warmth. "And that makes me wonder what it is you're hiding."

Millie's heart turned over, and it took everything in her to keep a smile pasted on her face.

"You're wasting your time, Tabitha. Really. There's nothing remotely interesting about Cal and me."

Tabitha hiked her expensive Gucci bag over her shoulder and moved past Millie Sue. "Isn't there?" she said as she headed toward the elevators. She stopped before pressing the button and turned around. "You should know a couple of things about me. I don't give up when I want something. I mean, I'll literally do whatever it takes to win. And I don't play by the rules. Smart people never do." She pressed the button, and the elevator doors slid open. "I'll see you soon." She walked into the elevator and turned to face Millie Sue. "Maybe at the Sundowner. I sure as heck don't want to miss another performance like last night's. Or maybe..." The doors started to slide shut. "I'll see you out at the ranch for Thanksgiving dinner."

With that, the woman disappeared from view, and Millie Sue let out a long, tortured breath she didn't even know she was holding in.

God, there wasn't a more despicable woman in Big Bend. How in hell had Bent started up with her in the first place?

Millie Sue took the stairs two at a time. She needed to burn off some steam. Or punch a wall. She thought of that woman's perfectly contoured nose. Maybe punch a face. By the time she reached the main floor, her blood was pounding, and the beginnings of a headache crept up her neck.

She was due at the bar, but no way was she ready to face questions and innuendo. There were a ton of messages on her phone she hadn't replied to and had no intention to. All to do with her stupidity the night before, no doubt. She slipped out her cell and sent a text to her cousin. Told him she was feeling under the weather and wouldn't be in unless it was absolutely necessary.

He replied in less than a minute.

All good. Jennifer is going to stay. She needs the extra $$ and I'll close if you take my shift tomorrow.

She sent back an affirmative, and, after staring at the phone, at the unread messages from Cal, and Taz and Mike Paul among others, she powered it down and climbed into her truck. She needed to unplug from everyone and pretend for just a little bit longer that her life hadn't taken a left turn the night before. Maybe she'd wake up in the morning and everything would be as it was before Cal had showed up in town.

A girl could hope, couldn't she?

CHAPTER 12

By Saturday evening, Cal had just about had it. He'd called Millie Sue more times than he could count, yet every single call went to voicemail. All his text messages were unanswered—in fact, they were *unread*—and as he stared into the darkness outside, a fire began in his belly. He'd never been a patient man, and damned if he was going to sit back and let her ignore him for no good reason.

He made a face at that thought because it was not exactly *no good reason*. He knew he should have stayed away from her but seeing Millie on stage had done something to him. It had made him remember all those nights they'd been up there together, making music and later making love. He didn't want to forget their history. Hell, if he was honest with himself, he'd love nothing more than to dive back into some of that and see where they ended up.

He'd thought of nothing but Millie Sue since Thursday night. The color of her hair, rich as aged cider, the curve of her cheek, the way her eyes sparkled when the lights hit them or flashed when she was angry with him.

"You got a weird look on your face."

He was in Bent's office, which had become a sanctuary of sorts, and glanced over to Ry, who stood with his hands shoved into the front of his jeans as he leaned against the doorframe. He hadn't seen him since dinner.

"Thought you had plans in town with your friends."

Ryland slid his long frame onto the seat by the fireplace. He slouched into it, the way most kids his age did, and shrugged. "Party got canceled. Trace's dad found out."

"Who's Trace?"

"Mulley. I think you know his uncle."

"Petey?"

Ryland nodded.

"I didn't know you hung out with that crew." As far as Cal remembered, the Mulley boys had always been in trouble for something or other.

"I don't, but Whit and the guys are out of town for football."

Cal studied his brother for a few moments and decided to poke his nose in where he knew Ryland didn't want it.

"Why'd you quit?" he asked. "You had a great arm and a love of the game. What changed?"

Ryland picked at some invisible thread on the edge of his T-shirt. "Guess I didn't like being told what to do all the time."

"I get that." Cal kept his tone conversational. "Football is a big commitment, and Coach Walters isn't the easiest man. Hell, I had more than my fair share of running extra laps or doing push-ups until I puked because I was a knucklehead and didn't listen."

"It's not even that. I just..." Ry seemed to be struggling with the right words. Just when Cal thought he was going to clam up, he spoke. "I didn't care about it. About any of it. The game. My friends. Carly. It's like none of that mattered because there was all this other stuff crowding it out."

"What kind of stuff?"

Ryland shrugged. "Just..." He swore and looked away. "Being a Bridgestone isn't always easy. People expect things. Good things. Bad things. I think I'm better at the bad things."

"Like drinking and crashing vehicles?"

Ry's head shot, and Cal noted the surprise. "Who told you?"

"It doesn't matter who told me. What matters is that there are people concerned about you." He waited a few seconds. "You going to tell me what happened?"

"Like you care."

"I do." That burn in his gut flamed something fierce, and he moved toward his brother. "I know it seems like I don't. Look, I can apologize for ghosting this family until my face turns blue, and it still won't be enough. I know I screwed up. I figured you were all okay. That Benton had everything in control."

"Well, you figured wrong," Ry shot back, clearly angry.

"I did. I got caught up in a life that's insane on any given day, and it was just easier to deal with that than worry about what was going on back here. I want you to know that if I had any inkling things were headed south, I would have come back sooner."

"And canceled your tour? Disappointed all those folks you seem to like more than us?"

What did Cal say to that? On some level, his brother was right. Cal Bridgestone the singer was a big machine, and there were a lot of cogs that made the wheels turn. He was responsible for the livelihoods of hundreds of people on his payroll. Canceling shows didn't just mean ticketholders were screwed, it meant that Dave, who worked behind the soundboard, or Janice, in charge of his light show, didn't get a paycheck, or any of the other men and women who worked his tour.

"I would have tried." His response sounded lame even to his own ears.

"Sometimes I think everything is crazy. Like all these pieces are moving so fast, but not clicking into the right place. Does that make sense?"

Cal slowly nodded. "Yes. I feel the same way sometimes. It's why I have Ivy pretty much running my life."

Ryland shook his head and looked away. "I don't want to be like Dad. Like how he was before. How I was when I got into that accident."

"You're aware that it could be a problem," Cal replied. "That's a good start."

"Is that why you hate him so much? Is Dad the reason you never came back?"

Shit. This conversation had taken a turn. He considered his answer and decided honesty was the way to go.

"He's part of it. A big part. After Mom died and the booze took over, he was the meanest drunk in the county. You were young, and we kept a lot from you. But you must have heard the fights. Seen the holes in the walls. The black eyes and bruises. I know he was hurting, but our dad took out his hurtin' on the ones he should have been protecting. I knew I had to get out, or one of us would end up dead."

Silence followed his words, and then Ryland moved so that he was straight and facing Cal. "You said he was only part of it. What was the other reason?"

Huh. Now they were entering real personal territory. The old Cal would have let it go and changed the subject, but Ryland looked so damn invested in this conversation, the first real conversation they'd had in years, that Cal kept the ball rolling. He was all in, and for once, it felt good and right.

"Millie Sue and I…we were having problems. I knew my head wasn't in Montana. Knew I wasn't gonna be a rancher like Bent, but she was on that path. She was talking about fixing up the Founder's Cabin and living there. Having babies and writing music and living life like there was no tomorrow. Her corner of the world was enough for her, and a part of me envied that, but the other part didn't understand it." He smiled, a small sad sort of thing as memories rolled across his brain like an old movie that had lost its color.

"She's so good, you know? Her voice is pure and unique and full of soul. Everything inside her spills out, and it's a fucking joy to listen to. To witness. She can hold a crowd in the palm of her hand like no one I've ever seen, including me. And on top of that, the girl can write." He grinned. "She was always doodling in notebooks, filling them up with drawings and words, and she'd make it all work and sound like magic. I never understood why she didn't want anyone to see it. To hear it. Why she was happy to play every weekend at her dad's place, or around a campfire with our friends, but nowhere else. It wasn't enough for me, and we fought about it until it ended us."

"She's real special," Ryland said, getting to his feet. "You love her."

"I…" Cal was speechless. Where the hell had the little punk-ass kid with the attitude gone? Ryland Bridgestone looked and sounded years older just then, and his gaze was direct as he chuckled.

"It's okay, bro. Love isn't a bad word. Especially for someone your age."

Love? Was he still in love with Millie Sue Jenkins? Cal swore and ran his hands across the stubble on his cheek as the band across his chest tightened. Had he ever *not* been in love with her? Wasn't it a fact that every long song he'd written had been about her? That all the women who'd come and gone in his life, the ones he'd used and left behind, had been a lame attempt to fill a hole only she could fill?

"Geez, you got it bad."

"What?" Cal said, staring across the room at his brother.

"Millie Sue."

There was no sense in denying it. "It seems to be a bit of a problem."

"Maybe you can make things work this time."

"Maybe."

"Though, knowing Mills, I bet she doesn't like you very much after that stunt you pulled on Thursday night."

"You heard about that," Cal said with a wry grin.

"Who hasn't? It's still trending everywhere. No one cares about Swift and Kelce anymore. It's all about Bridgestone and the mystery woman. I heard there were strangers in town asking about her."

"What?" Shit. Cal had more than a problem on his hands. He needed to get hold of Ivy. She'd be able to fix it.

Ryland turned to leave the room. "Normally, Mills doesn't work Saturday nights at the Sundowner, but I know for a fact she's closing tonight."

At Cal's raised eyebrow, Ryland shrugged. "I have a buddy who works in the kitchen. Maybe you should pay her a visit to see how mad she is."

"Maybe you should give Carly a call and let her know you haven't forgotten her."

"Maybe." Ryland cracked a smile, and then his kid brother was gone.

Left alone once again, and restless as hell, Cal checked his phone and noted it was nearly midnight. If he headed to town now, he'd get to the Sundowner before last call. He fingered his cell once more, saw all the unread messages, and thought *fuck it*. Couldn't hurt. He sent a message to Ivy and, decision made, grabbed his jacket and headed out into the cold, crisp November night.

It was time he started mending some of those fences he'd let fall down.

CHAPTER 13

Millie Sue locked the door behind Jennifer. She took a few moments to just breathe, then turned around and let her gaze wander the now-empty bar. She was in a weird place. Tired as hell because she hadn't slept much the last few nights, but wired and jumpy. It had been a busy night. A lot of folks had come out thinking there would be a repeat performance of Thursday night, but she'd quickly dashed everyone's hopes by staying behind the bar—and the fact that one bona fide country superstar had been a no-show pretty much put a nail in that coffin.

A part of her thought Cal would drop by, but every time the door flew open, it was some other man who appeared. And she was fine with that, because she wasn't in the right head space for Cal Bridgestone.

It *should* bother her. How much she thought of him. How much she wanted to see him even though she was still mad as hell. Big Bend had been invaded by paparazzi, of all things. Here. In this town out in the middle of Nowhere, Montana. She'd had Taz escort three different men out of the bar because they'd been trying to take her photo without permission, while asking all sorts of inappropriate questions. She wasn't used to that crap and resented the hell out of the fact that the Sundowner had been invaded by men looking to profit off a picture or juicy gossip. Men who didn't belong in her corner of the world.

Yet, as the silence wrapped itself around her, Millie found herself drifting in a wash of nostalgia and melancholy. So much so that she found herself heading for the jukebox, her tired body suddenly as wired as her brain. She wasn't sure how long she stared down at the thing, but eventually, she leaned against the machine and dug into the front pocket of her jeans until she found a quarter. The jukebox was as old as the Sundowner and still loaded with all the original tunes that were now classics. She deposited the coin and chose the same song she always did when she was alone and feeling blue, a ballad by Patsy Cline that tugged on every heartstring she owned.

The lights were low, and the smell of beer and fried food permeated the air, like every other honkytonk she'd ever been in. Smell was memory, and as Patsy began to sing, Millie Sue swayed to the melody, singing along and harmonizing with a woman who'd been dead for decades. Her words, the power of her voice, was still very much alive, and her crazy longing for a man who didn't love her back was as palpable this night as it was the day Cline recorded it.

The last note lingered, and, surprised, Millie swiped at tears that stung the corners of her eyes. Would this feeling ever go away? Would she always be half happy and half sad? Could she live the rest of her life like this?

"My God, Mills, get your head on straight." Her voice was raw.

A tapping noise caught her attention, and she whipped around, fear rising when she spied a shadow outside the door. The upper section was frosted glass, so it was easy to see. Whoever it was, was big. Heart pounding, she dug into her pants for her phone, but realized it was in the office. *Shit.* Was it one of the men Taz had escorted out of the bar earlier in the night?

She was just about to run back to the office and retrieve her phone when she heard him, his voice like a whisper in her head.

"It's me, Mills."

Cal.

"Can we talk?"

Her heart had to be in her ears because it was all she heard. Thump-thump-thump in rapid succession. Breaths falling like stones, she walked toward the door, though she paused an inch or so away. Long moments passed, and neither of them spoke, Cal out in the cold, and Millie Sue frozen on the other side.

"Millie?"

She knew this was wrong. Letting him in. But Millie seemed helpless to stop herself. She reached for the door, unlocked it, and stepped back.

Cal strode into the Sundowner, and she clicked the bolt behind him. She didn't turn around, but rested her head against the door, unwilling to face this man who affected her like no one else ever would.

"Hey," he said softly.

"Hey," she replied. She swallowed and faced him. He looked so damn good, it made her heart ache. Thick wavy hair curled around his neck, and there was more than a five o'clock shadow darkening his jaw. His navy-blue eyes were electric, seemingly luminous in the low lights. And that mouth of his was curved into a half smile. It hurt just to look at him.

"I was in the parking lot for an hour." His voice was low. "Wasn't sure if I should come in."

Millie exhaled and decided to deflect. "You want a drink?"

"You still serving?"

"Technically, we're closed, but I suppose I could be persuaded." Holy. Mary. Mother. Of. God. When had she turned in the flirty fairy of Big Bend?

His answer was that dimple on the right as his smile deepened. "I could handle whiskey over ice." He moved off toward the jukebox. As he shoveled in some coins, Millie got busy behind the bar.

She grabbed two glasses and filled them with ice, then reached for her special bottle of Forty Creek, a Canadian whiskey her father had always loved. She poured a generous amount in each and then pushed one of the glasses toward Cal, who'd sat himself down on the stool directly in front of her.

He reached for the glass, his long fingers easily closing around it, and brought it to his mouth. Millie didn't realize she'd been holding her breath until he tipped the glass back. She let it out in a rush and knocked back half of hers in one gulp. She gripped the edge of the bar as the liquid burned its way down, those subtle notes of caramel, vanilla, and butterscotch making her senses sing. No longer was she tired or muddled. In fact, every cell in her body was on fire. As she took another sip, she knew she could drink this whiskey all night, but it wouldn't come close to quenching the kind of thirst she felt.

An old Hank Williams song filled the silence of the big room, the legend's voice both plaintive and cajoling. For the longest time, the two of them politely sipped from their glasses, listening to Hank talk about a woman who did him wrong, then Cash lament about Folsom Prison.

Eventually, Cal pushed his now-empty tumbler toward her. Millie refilled it without speaking. Her heart was beating so damn loud, she was sure Cal heard it. Skin hot, her white tank top clung to her. She had no idea what it was they were doing, but she knew it was something. No longer were they skimming the edge of what had been. This felt new.

And that's what scared her.

He sat back, his expression unreadable. When he spoke, it was almost anticlimactic.

"I'm sorry about Thursday. About the attention I brought to you. I know it's not your thing and I should have known better, but in the moment, I wasn't thinking about any of that." He paused and downed the rest of his whiskey. "In that moment, all I was thinking about was you and how good it feels to be near you. To listen to you. Watch you come alive. It was like we'd walked back in time, and I guess I let it carry me away." A ghost of a smile touched his lips, and he shrugged. "You were always special, Mills. The kind of special that doesn't come along often. And to see that again? Well, I'm not sorry about that." He shook his head. "Not sorry at all."

Millie lowered her eyes and focused on the glass in her hands. The air was thick, and she had difficulty breathing. Or maybe it was the melody of memory in her head, the idea of the two of them that made her tongue thick.

"Are we good?" he asked.

She nodded but didn't trust herself to speak. How was it, after all this time, she still felt like that sixteen-year-old schoolgirl standing in front of a boy who, with one look, could make her forget a world existed outside the two of them?

"Can you say something?" he prodded, leaning forward, a slight frown touching his forehead.

There was so much she could say. Tell him to leave. Or he could stay and she would go home. She could tell him that there hadn't been anyone who'd come close to claiming the part of her that still belonged to him. She could let him know that she'd finally forgiven him for leaving all those years ago. Because really, how could she hate the man she loved for chasing his dreams? Wasn't that what love really meant? Letting someone go?

She blinked at the thought. At how true it was.

In the end, all those things stayed safe inside her soul. Locked away until it was time. But for now, there were other things on her mind. Hot things. Dark things. Needful things.

"I miss you," she breathed, still staring at her glass, aware that every cell in her body felt electrified. She was aware of movement. Of Cal sliding off the stool and making his way around the bar until he stood inches from her.

Still, she kept her eyes down, afraid he'd see into her very soul. She felt his hand on her chin, and all resistance melted away. Slowly, she raised her head—she had nowhere to hide anymore.

"Do you remember when we were seventeen and we took that raft onto the river, thinking we'd drift for a couple of hours and drink some of the beers I'd stolen from Dad?"

She smiled at the memory. Leaned into that big warm hand at her cheek. "It was the perfect afternoon. There's no place like Montana in July."

"We drifted until we spotted the Founder's Cabin."

Entangled limbs. Naked skin. Hot, young, first love. It had been her first time.

He bent closer, and she froze. In that moment, she saw everything. His heart. His mind. His conflict. His *love*. All of it. She knew this wasn't casual, an old lover reuniting with a flame to see if the fire was still hot. This was real. He felt it. And so did she.

With a soft groan, she took a step back, unsure. Millie knew what she wanted to do. Her body ached for his touch. God, it had been so long. But if she gave in...if she started up with Cal Bridgestone, it wouldn't end well. He would leave again. In spite of his love.

Would she survive it a second time?

She thought about that. About how she'd been living only half a life. She went through the motions of day to day, did and said all the right things. She was there for her friends, for what little family she had, but at night when she was home alone, she was empty. She had nothing for herself.

I want the well filled, she thought. Even if it was only for a short time.

That right there was the difference between now and sixteen. Between a girl and a woman. No longer was she young or naive—she knew the score. And it was up to her to decide if the consequence was worth it.

"Mills?" His voice was like crack. Like the deadliest drug on the planet and it had been too long since her last fix.

"I want you," she said simply.

He looked surprised, and that made her smile. As if him walking through the door thirty minutes ago wasn't leading to this.

"Are you sure?" He moved closer, his hands on either side of her face.

"No," she whispered, leaning up for his mouth. "But that's okay."

Her hands splayed across his chest, and she felt his heart beating as fast and as hard as hers. When his lips skimmed her mouth, electric bolts slid across her skin and she groaned, immediately opening up for him. He tasted like whiskey and spice. His mouth was demanding as he gripped Millie tightly, kissing her until her head spun.

That was the thing about Cal Bridgestone. He's always known how to kiss. How to touch. How to excite. This was no fumbling Joe looking to score a touchdown, but a man who knew how to take his time. Cal had always been a generous lover. Even that first time on the dock by the Founder's Cabin, with nothing but the wilds of Montana to watch.

He cupped her ass and pulled her closer still, so there was no mistaking his desire. With a strangled noise, he pulled away, and she frowned, hating the loss of his touch. Cal rested his forehead against hers, breaths ragged as he tried to gain some kind of control.

"I didn't come here for this," he managed to say.

"I call bullshit."

He smiled, and those blue eyes of his glistened. "I mean, I might have hoped, but I didn't think this was where we were headed." His grin widened. "Just yet." He held her gaze, a forefinger tracing her lips, swollen from his own. "Tell me now. Say the words and I'll stop. I'll get in my truck and go home, and I won't bother you again."

This was it. The precipice she'd been so damn afraid of. She either jumped or stepped back. She moved closer and pressed her most intimate self against him and blew out a long breath.

"I want you to stay."

"I don't have anything on me."

It took a bit for his words to penetrate. For their meaning to become clear.

"I'm on the pill and, well," she said, "I'm clean, if that's what you're wondering."

"I'm good in that area." His voice was rough, and she knew he was as close to the edge as she was.

Millie Sue couldn't think about right or wrong or consequences and bad choices. All she knew was that in this moment, Cal felt right. *They* felt right. She knew it wouldn't last. Of course, it wouldn't.

But damned if she was giving him up just yet.

CHAPTER 14

In his lifetime, Cal had been 100% right about a few things. One, he'd known that if he left Big Bend and found a way to get his music out into the world, he would make something of himself. Two, he'd be half happy doing it. And three...Millie Sue Jenkins pulled every damn string he owned.

And then some.

In fourth grade when she'd punched Dale McGlintock in the face for pulling up Ivy's dress in the church parking lot, he'd taken notice. After that, they'd been pals. She was almost a year younger, but more than able to keep up with all the rough-and-tumble boys he hung with—Mike Paul among them. They'd fish and ride in the summer, play ball and spend afternoons at the pond swimming and jumping from the rope. When his mother died, she'd been the ear he sought, the one who gave the hugs and comfort he'd needed.

When his father had used his alcohol-infused fists to express his feelings, his discontent and unhappiness with the world, she'd been the only one he'd confided in. They'd been close. So close that other than Mike Paul, he considered her to be his best friend.

The year she turned sixteen, Millie Sue had been packed off to California for four months visiting family and a mother she barely knew. He'd missed her, and though they'd shared weekly phone calls, Angel Saunders had helped pass the time. Within a couple of weeks, he'd made it past third base, and all he could think about was Angel, getting naked, and having sex.

The phone calls to Millie had grown sparse, and they didn't speak the last month she was away. When she showed up for tenth grade, her sophomore year, she had breasts and a butt that didn't quit, along with an anger toward him he didn't quite understand.

Angel wasn't his girlfriend, though that didn't seem to matter to Millie. She ignored him completely, which was a problem because she was all he could think about. Him and every other rambunctious boy in school.

Without realizing it, he began to woo the young spitfire with hair the color of dark rust and eyes that matched the sky. Slowly, her artic frost thawed. The Bridgestone charm was legendary, and they settled into something like what they'd been before. Only this time, there was an undercurrent of feelings they didn't quite know how to deal with.

Music became a big part of their lives, and it had brought them closer together. How many nights had they spent under the stars, around a campfire with their guitars and friends, singing songs by the greats? Waylon, Cash, and Hank... Too many to count and all of them burned into his memory.

Then they'd taken that trip down the river when they were seventeen. It was there everything had changed. It was there he'd claimed every part of Millie Sue. She'd stamped herself across his heart with the kind of ferocity only the young and naive knew. Given herself to him with the pureness of first love.

It was a love he'd eventually destroyed.

Since he'd left Big Bend, there'd been a lot of women, a few he'd even dated longer than a few weeks, but none had come close to Millie Sue Jenkins. As Cal gazed down at her kiss-swollen lips, he realized that none ever would.

I still love her.

He was, as the boys would say, absolutely fucked, and yet he didn't care. All he could think of was that he needed her to be inside her with a hurt that wouldn't quit.

Cal gently lifted her into his arms and set her on the bar. She immediately opened her legs, and he settled himself between them, sliding his mouth up along her neck. She shivered, and he smiled wickedly, his tongue licking along the base where her pulse beat rapidly.

It matched the rhythm of his own, but he clamped down on his desire as best he could and continued to tease his way up to her mouth once more, then claimed her in a kiss that had her moaning and writhing beneath him.

Cal liked this. The kissing. Sure, it made him as hard as a rock, uncomfortably so, but hell, pleasure and pain worked better together. He pushed her back a bit so that she had to use her hands to grip the edge of the bar and gently pushed up her tank top, then reached around and unsnapped her bra.

"Still got that move," she breathed against him. Her tongue was still caught in her teeth when sat back, and he took in the hottest sight he'd ever seen. Her breasts were perfect, not too big, not too small, just enough to fill his large hands. Her nipples were erect, the deep-rose buds begging for him, and as he closed his mouth over one of them, she hissed and swore, her hands no longer on the bar, but buried deep in the hair at his nape.

"You still like my moves," he murmured, tugging with his teeth, then blowing on her nipples before suckling them.

"Well," she managed to say, "they are a bit rusty."

He chuckled, his hands gently massaging her breasts as he continued to lick and suckle until she swore and threw her head back. Her hips gyrated slowly, and he smelled her arousal through her jeans. The scent pulled at that animal part of him, and he had her jeans undone and pulled down past her knees before she had a chance to react.

Cal had to slow down or he was going to blow things before he had a chance to cross the finish line. He took a moment, exhaled slowly.

"You gonna take all day down there, chief?"

He ripped off her boots in answer along with the jeans, leaving her in nothing but a black thong. Her hair hung down past her shoulders, her skin flushed a rosy pink, and she smiled wickedly, widening her legs a tad more, giving him the access he needed.

Cal liked to use his hands, and he began a slow, methodical massage starting at her toes and working his way up. By the time he reached her thighs, her legs quivered and her chest rose and fell rapidly.

He slid his hands around her butt and pulled her closer to the edge, claiming her mouth as he did so.

"Why am I naked and you're still wearing all those clothes?" she asked breathlessly against his mouth.

"Because this is about you, Mills." He deepened the kiss, smiling against her mouth when she started making those little noises he'd missed so damn much. "I haven't even gotten to the good stuff."

"What are you waiting for?"

His hand shot between her legs, and he slowly massaged the hot triangle of thin silky material.

"Cal," she said, her voice rough. "Just like that."

"You're so fucking wet," he growled against her mouth. "For me."

"For you," she breathed.

He grazed her nipples once more and then ripped her thong, tossing it to the floor. She was open, glistening for him. His cock ached like a son of a bitch, and it took everything Cal had not to take it out and sink into her, but he had other plans.

Gently, he parted her folds, nearly blowing his load when he spied her engorged clitoris. He bent forward, smiling when she hissed at his touch, and flicked his tongue over it, inhaling her scent and savoring it.

She was a drug, and he was an addict.

Cal buried his face in her pussy, holding her steady with his hands on either side of her hips, while he licked and sucked and teased and ate at the bounty in front of him. She bucked and yelled, her body quivering as the first wave of an orgasm rolled through her. He licked up every bit of it and continued to torture her until she crashed again.

"I can't, Cal. Oh my God," she managed to say, hands releasing his head as she exhaled. She caught her breath, her eyes widening when she dropped her gaze to his crotch. Slowly, a smile slid across her face, and she widened her legs even more, her fingers now replacing his as she began to play with herself, slowly rolling over her clit and disappearing inside.

He was done. His eyes saw red. His cock begged for release.

He didn't say anything. He grabbed her and carried her to the nearest table. With one swipe of his arm, he unloaded condiments and whatever the hell else was there. She lay back, this Jezebel he craved like no other, and he unzipped, let his jeans fall to give him room to maneuver, and before either of them could ponder whether this was a good idea or not, he buried his cock inside her.

Damn.

Tight. Wet. Warm.

Cal had to take a moment because he was so close to the finish line, he knew he'd blow before she had a chance to join him. But the little devil wasn't having any of it. She began to gyrate, to make those fucking noises again—the ones that drove him crazy—and he slowly began to move. He might be near to finishing, but he was going to make sure she enjoyed every last second of it for as long as he could go.

"Faster," she growled.

"No," he managed to say before capturing her mouth once more and inhaling any other words she had. He plundered her mouth as his cock filled her. The taste and touch and smell of Millie was an aphrodisiac that, if bottled, would make him a billionaire. He couldn't get enough, and yet he held on, slowly pulling out before plunging back in again. He did that until she bit him, and he laughed, hands on her head now so he could hold her steady as he increased his rhythm.

"You're driving me crazy," she said, matching him, her hips moving faster.

"Same," he said through clenched teeth, his shirt now soaked through with sweat.

"Cal, was it always this good?" Her voice ended on a yelp, and he knew he'd hit that special spot. One hand holding her hips at an angle, he increased his thrusts, the intensity built to drive them both home.

He watched her, this beautiful woman who gave herself up to him with no agenda, withholding nothing. When her eyes slammed shut and she tightened around him, he finally let go, his hands dug in, his body covering hers fully.

They came together in a tangled mess of slick skin, scorching kisses, and an orgasm that shook him to the core. He had no idea how long it lasted. Only that when the red haze cleared, and his body was spent, he stroked her cheek and dropped one last kiss to her mouth.

"In answer to your question," he said hoarsely, "I don't it's ever been that good."

She licked her bottom lip and sighed. "Maybe we should try again? Just to be sure."

Cal cracked a smile. "Give me ten minutes and we'll see."

"You need that much?" She sat up and slid off the table, Cal already hard at the sight of her completely naked in the bar. Love bites marked the side of her neck and her breasts, and she cupped them, running her fingers along the nipples, her eyes wide and glistening as she looked at him.

"Five should do," he growled, reaching for his shirt. He pulled it over his head, and it was game on.

CHAPTER 15

It was Sunday, late afternoon, and Millie was in the kitchen, humming some mindless tune while munching on a potato chip, Mr. Higgins snuggled on the sofa. Outside, darkness touched the edge of a snow-filled sky that promised another dumping; up to ten inches, according to the local news.

She had a pot of chili on the stove, fresh bread just out of the oven, and her stomach rumbled at the aroma. She wasn't much of a cook, but man, she made a mean chili. Her hair was pulled up into a loose knot, and she wrinkled her nose as a strand tickled the end of it. Millie stretched and grimaced, swearing under her breath as she rubbed along her back and down her thighs. She was sore. Ached in places that hadn't ached in a long, long time.

But damn, it had been worth it.

She blushed at the thought of her and Cam in the Sundowner. Having sex everywhere. The bar. The table. Up against the wall near the stage. On the stage. They'd behaved like two horny teenagers who'd just discovered what happens when you insert A into B and have at it.

Then they'd locked up and come back to her place. She'd woken up to Cal inside her, his hands holding her in place as he moved from behind. He'd rocked into Millie until she couldn't see straight, and then they'd had sex one last time in the shower before he'd had to leave. He was, after all, now a responsible adult and had Nora, Ryland, and Scarlett waiting for him at home.

There were no words about love or any of that kind of stuff. No way were those three words falling from her lips. But there'd been tender moments when eyes connected and fingers caressed. It was as if they didn't want to talk about what they were feeling. About how this would affect their relationship.

Whatever that meant.

A knock at the door banished all thoughts of the night before, and with a quick rotation of her shoulders, the kink in her neck lessened. Millie crossed the room and threw open the door, letting in a gust of wind and a hint of snow. She stepped back when she spied Ivy standing there, a big bag of popcorn in one hand and an overnight bag in the other.

Ivy sailed past her, long hair loose and curling over her thick black puffer coat, a canary-yellow wool hat on top of her head. She set down her bag of snacks, dropped her backpack, and turned to Millie, a dramatic flourish to her hands as she flicked them toward her, eyebrows raised. She pushed up her glasses and cocked her head to the side.

"You and Cal," Ivy said.

There was no point denying it, so Millie just smiled and enveloped her old friend in a hug.

Ivy made a hilarious gesture of sniffing Millie's neck. "You've had *all* the sex."

"Not all."

"Most of it," Ivy shot back.

"You're just jealous," Millie replied lightly.

"You got that right," Ivy lamented, doffing her coat and hat. "It's been so long, I don't think I remember how to do it."

"That's what I thought until last night." Millie giggled. "Though it's true what they say."

"What's that?" Ivy asked, helping herself to a glass of water.

"It's like riding a bike." She winked. "Or ringing a bell."

"Well, my bike hasn't been ridden in so long, I swear I feel like a virgin again, and I haven't rung a bell since the tag races in seventh grade."

"If the right bike comes along..."

Ivy raised her glass in a toast. "The right bike hasn't come along in forever. I swear the only relationship I've had of late is with my vibrator."

Millie grabbed an empty glass and clinked it with Ivy's. "To vibrators."

"To vibrators," Ivy echoed.

"And old lovers." Millie filled her glass with orange juice, eyes on her friend. "Before we get into the inevitable tongue spanking you're dying to give me, I've been wondering where you've been. I expected to see you days ago."

Ivy shrugged. "I had things to do, some tour stuff to deal with and a few other commitments Cal had. This tour is on a scale we haven't done before, and there are a lot of working parts to rearrange."

"Mike Paul was asking. I think he's a little miffed you didn't come and see him right away."

"Please," she replied dismissively. "He's too busy with every single woman in Big Bend. I ran into him today. Like literally. He was coming out of the Coffee Hut with Laney

Bancroft. That woman has been divorced for less than a month, and already he's keeping her company."

"She's just a distraction." Millie knew Mike Paul would be a hard man to tame for any woman. He had more charm in his pinky finger than most people could hope to gain in a lifetime.

"We had coffee." Ivy made a face. "He told me about Trish and Samantha. Apparently, they're keeping him company too. That boy never changes. Can't he ever settle on one female?"

"Not as long as women are willing to share him." Millie laughed and joined her friend at the kitchen island. She grabbed a nacho chip and dug into the bowl of salsa with gusto. "The girls know what he's all about, and as long as they're willing to play his game, I can't see him stopping." She raised an eyebrow. "You ever meet a man who would turn down sex?"

"Does that animal even exist?"

The girls spent the next few hours catching up on life. They'd always kept in touch, a text message here, a phone call there, but Millie Sue hadn't seen Ivy in person since her father's funeral. She told Ivy how busy she was with the Sundowner and how much she loved living in this house in the middle of a Montana paradise. She mentioned volunteering a few times a month at the wildlife rescue and rehabilitation center outside of town, and that she tried to attend church every now and again because she knew it would make her father happy.

In return, Ivy told a few funny stories about living on the road and gave great details about some of the amazing places she'd visited, including the Australian Outback, the Leaning Tower of Pisa, and Belize. To her credit, she didn't mention Cal once. Millie knew it was coming, but she sure as hell wasn't going to bring it up.

Ivy opened a bottle of wine, a rich Pinot Noir, and once their glasses were filled, they moved to the sofa in front of the fireplace.

"So," Ivy said softly. "This Taz guy, who's he?"

Surprised at the question, Millie shrugged. "Just a friend. He was a big deal on the rodeo circuit a few years back, but his sister and her husband passed in a bad accident." She paused. "Do you remember Matt Weaver?" At Ivy's nod, she continued. "His sister Jenna married him."

"That's so sad," Ivy murmured.

"Yes. Taz came out right away. They had no one else."

"He sounds like a saint."

"Far from it." Millie grinned. "But he's a great guy."

"There's nothing between you, then? Because I heard there was."

Millie blushed when she thought of how she'd coerced Taz into pretending to mean something to her, which obviously hadn't lasted longer than a day or so.

"No. He's just a good friend." Her eyes widened as she looked at her friend, an idea forming. "He's hot."

"I heard that too."

"Single."

"Sounding better."

"Could be the one to help you with that bike riding problem."

Ivy giggled at that. "I doubt I'll be in town long enough to work my way up to that. I'm not really a one-night-stand kind of girl, but thanks for thinking of me."

Millie's smile faded a bit, and she nodded. "Right. When do you head back on tour?"

Ivy swished the wine in her glass. "Not until after the New Year. We rescheduled Cal's Australian dates and his other European stops. We'll be pretty busy mid-January through to the summer with breaks here and there." She paused, eyebrow raised. "About you and Cal. Are you sure it's a good idea?"

"Hell, no," Millie replied lightly. Her chin quivered, and suddenly, a wave of emotion rolled over her. She lowered her gaze and picked at the edge of the sofa. "I can't seem to help myself."

Ivy reached over and gave her a hug. "Just so you know, I'm pretty sure he feels the same. He's never been with anyone longer than a minute. Not in the entire time he's been away from Big Bend. He's never met anyone like you." She sat back. "He's not looking."

"He's too busy to look, but one day, he'll find someone who fits into his life." She shrugged. "You and I both know it's not me."

"I wouldn't be so quick to say that, Mills. It's like the two of you fit in a way that's special." She sank back on the sofa. "God, that video. I mean, watching the two of you together was like, like it was always supposed to be that way. I just wish you could..."

"Could what?" Millie asked.

"Figure out how to make it work?"

"That will never happen. I won't leave Big Bend, and he won't stay. I never quite understood his need to leave, and he couldn't understand why I couldn't. I don't want to live away from this place. Suitcases and hotels are not for me. I need room to roam. I'm happy with simple. With Big Bend and the view from my window. I'm happy singing to the crowd at my bar when I feel like it, writing songs for myself and no one else. Cal needs so much more than that. This county isn't big enough for him. Hell, the entire state doesn't even come close."

Ivy digested her words and then whispered, "I'm sorry."

"Don't be," Millie Sue replied, attempting a smile that fell flat. "I've learned that you can love someone with all your heart, but you're not supposed to be with them. Cal is that person to me."

"How does that make you happy?"

"It doesn't really."

Ivy shook her head. "How do you live that way?"

Millie sighed and took another sip from her wineglass. "When I figure that out, I'll let you know." She jumped to her feet. "Can we change the subject? Cal Bridgestone isn't a part of this girl's night. I don't want to talk about him anymore. Let's eat some chocolate, lament the sad state of our love lives, and figure out a way for you to get back on the bike."

Ivy held up her empty glass.

"You had me at chocolate."

CHAPTER 16

SUNDAY EVENING BROUGHT WITH IT A FRESH DUMPING OF snow that made Triple B Ranch look like a picture-perfect postcard for Montana tourism. Cal and Ryland had spent most of the day helping Dallas and the ranch hands take feed out to the cattle—large bales of hay to help supplement any grazing now underneath the white stuff.

It had been a long time since he'd gotten his hands dirty and worked a physical shift, and as far as Cal was concerned it beat hitting the gym any day. He missed it. Being out in the open air, working with the animals, hanging with the men who made the entire operation work. None of them treated him differently. To them, he was just a Bridgestone who worked the ranch, not a singer or celebrity or any of that. It was refreshing. Afterward, they'd cooked up some steaks and, with full bellies and a couple of cold beers, spent too much time reminiscing about their younger years.

He felt light. Like a part of his soul had been replenished. Cal knew it was more than being on the ranch. It was because of Millie Sue.

He couldn't stop thinking about her. About the other

night and all the things they'd done. He smiled at the thought.

"You look funny again." Startled, he cleared his throat and looked down at his niece.

It was Monday morning, and because of the snow, instead of taking Nora to school, Cal was getting the little princess out into the winter wonderland, with the intention of chopping down a Christmas tree. Thanksgiving was only days away, and according to Mackenzie, Benton could come home on Wednesday if he continued to improve.

Cal meant for it to be the best Thanksgiving the Bridgestones had seen in years. He had Rose grabbing all the food and fixings they'd need and had wrangled some of her best recipes, including the green bean casserole with honeyed ham. It had been a while since he'd tackled cooking, but hell, considering he had Ryland and Scarlett to help, the outcome couldn't be that bad.

"Do I have to wear my brown boots?" Nora stared up at him, cheeks flushed with excitement, thought a small pout touched her lips. "I want to wear my cowboy boots."

"Those aren't warm enough."

"But I like them better." She glared down at the practical boots on her feet and made a face. "These don't have any sparkles."

God. His niece was the girliest girl on the planet. How in hell Bent had managed to raise a daughter who thought rhinestones and glitter were the best things ever, Cal had no idea. He glanced up at the cubby above the coat rack and spied a pink scarf with shiny threads of silver and emerald running through it. He grabbed it and wound it around Nora's right boot, tying it tightly. Then tried not to smile at the dubious look on her face as she rotated her foot.

"It sparkles in the light," he said cajolingly as he straightened.

"Not super bright," she said, but he knew he'd won this particular battle. "I guess it's okay."

"I'm coming too." They both looked up as Ryland walked into the mud room. At the look of surprise on Cal's face, the teen shrugged. "Carly was supposed to come over, but she's not dug out yet. Besides, I know where the best trees are."

Cal didn't point out the fact he already knew this. Instead, he pulled on a hat and grabbed his gloves.

"We taking the sleds?" Ryland asked. At Cal's nod, he headed outside. "I'll bring them up from the shed."

Nora helped Cal pack a bag of snacks and water. His and Ry's contained granola bars, ham sandwiches, and fruit, while Nora's had a bag of Froot Loops and a caramel candy apple that was left over from Halloween. He wasn't sure they'd need the food, but the Montana wilderness could be an unforgiving place, and he'd learned at a young age that you had to be prepared whenever venturing out into it. He grabbed the shotgun from the cabinet, and they joined his brother outside. Scarlett was still in bed, and though Cal was more than a little worried about her, he knew she was dealing with some heavy things and needed time to work her way through them.

She'd come around. With a baby on the way, she had to.

Ryland led the way toward high country, and with little Nora sitting in front of Cal, pretending she was driving the snowmobile, he followed behind. The sun was high, brilliant, and so bright they needed their goggles. Without a cloud to mar its blue perfection, the sky seemed an endless horizon.

It took a couple of hours to get to where suitably sized

Douglas fir grew, and by the time Nora trekked through a patch of them, it was nearly an hour after that. She sang along as she hopped from tree to tree and finally picked one for Cal to cut down. He got out the axe, and with Nora off following a rabbit trail, Ryland keeping track behind, Cal cut down the tree, covered it in burlap, and then secured it to the back of his sled.

By now, it was early afternoon, and they had an hour or so before they'd need to head back to the house. Hot from all the chopping, he slipped out of his coat and leaned back against the sled, munching on a granola bar. He was about to dig into a sandwich when movement caught his eye. He paused, narrowing his gaze on a patch of darkness that slithered between the stand of pine off to his right.

Unease slid through him. Cal slowly eased himself up off the sled—his shotgun was in its holder on the other side. Snow had begun to fall, big fat flakes that had come from nowhere, making it hard to see exactly what was out there.

He heard a low rumble and swore silently as he looked over his shoulder at his rifle. He leaned back and managed to grab it just as a growl made the hair on the back of his neck stand on end. A lone wolf peered at him from the shadows, a big animal from the looks of it. Carefully, he readied the shotgun in case he needed it.

Cal was more than a little nervous. He hadn't shot one in a long time.

Seconds ticked by as he and the wolf stared at each other, until they were both startled when Nora came crashing into the clearing, her squeals accompanied by her gleeful voice.

"Uncle Cal, I'm catching snowflakes on my tongue. Look!" The little girl in the parka had her face raised to the sky, tongue lolling out. "Can you see it?" she shouted.

The wolf took two steps forward, and Cal raised the rifle, his heart pounding at the thought of something hurting her. He exhaled slowly, had a clear shot, when Nora shouted once more.

"Penny, you silly girl. What are you doing there?"

Astonished, he took a step forward, unsure, as the large wolf bounded toward the girl and accepted her hug without pause. The animal turned its head toward Cal as if to say *dumbass* in a sarcastic way, and then ignored him completely.

Cal placed the rifle back in its holder and grabbed his cell. No one was going to believe this. He took several photos and had just put his phone away when Ryland walked toward him, arms laden with greenery.

"For the stairs," he mumbled, walking by Nora and the wolf as if it wasn't weird to see his little niece playing with a hundred-pound wolf. His brother unpacked their sandwiches, and they ate in silence, watching the little girl roll around in the snow, and giggle like a hyena.

"You're sure the wolf is good with her?" Cal asked, dubiously.

"Penny would protect Nora with her life." Ryland shrugged. "They're bonded. We all are. It's like we're part of Penny's pack."

"She's far from the cabin."

"She'll go back to him. She always does."

"She'll mate one day." Cal studied his brother. "Then she'll be gone."

Ryland shrugged. "I guess everyone leaves." He finished his sandwich and crumpled up the paper it had been wrapped in. "What's it like being away from here? Like on tour and everything."

"It's busy," Cal replied, thinking about the tour that had

just abruptly ended. "Our production is huge, and we've got a lot of folks working it. Most of them have been with me since the beginning. Since that first tour nearly ten years ago."

"You must love it." Ryland glanced at him. "To not come back to this."

Cal was taken aback. He'd never really thought of it in those terms. As he looked around at this slice of Montana heaven, an ached formed in his chest.

"You know me being here is complicated," he admitted.

Ryland made a face. "I know you have issues with Dad. I know you have issues with Millie Sue. What I don't know is why you can't fix them."

"It's complicated."

"That's what adults say when they don't want to talk about something."

Cal didn't quite know how to answer his brother, but luckily, he didn't need to.

"I want Dad to be there on Thursday." Ryland glanced over at him. "For Thanksgiving dinner. He needs to be there when Benton comes home."

Cal's initial response, a quick denial, died on his tongue when Nora squealed. "Papa is coming to dinner. Yay! Can he bring Penny?" She'd dragged the wolf over by its snout, and the two of them stood inches from Cal, Nora grinning and the wolf watching him intently.

"I don't know about the wolf," Cal said slowly. "But yes, your Papa will be there and so will your daddy."

"Oh," she said, her face suddenly serious, "this is the bestest day ever. Did you hear that, Penny? Daddy is coming home." She hugged the wolf fiercely before turning back to Cal. "Are we decorating the tree tonight?"

"I'll get the tree up and ready, but why don't we do the

decorating Wednesday when your dad is home? Don't you think he'd like that?"

Nora nodded excitedly.

"We have a plan," he said, thinking it gave him a couple more days to convince Millie Sue to join them. He smiled at the thought.

"You have that funny look again, Uncle Cal."

He ignored the all-seeing eyes of his niece and turned to Ryland. "We should go, or we'll get caught out here in the dark."

He and Ryland got themselves sorted on their sleds, and they took off for home. Cal wasn't sure how long Penny ran alongside them, but eventually, she melted into the shadows, most likely headed back to the Founder's Cabin.

By the time they made it home, it was dusk, and as he walked into the house, he couldn't shake what fell over him like an old friend. A feeling. A notion.

It almost felt like home again.

CHAPTER 17

Tuesday afternoon found Millie Sue at the Sundowner, taking delivery of all the stuff that hadn't come the day before on account of the storm. The bar was empty, save for two tables at the back, a couple enjoying hamburgers and fries, and old Mr. Bennet sitting alone in his favorite booth, sipping from the same mug of draft beer she'd poured him ninety minutes earlier.

Millie's favorite country station was on, and as Cal's latest single, *You Ain't Nothing but Trouble,* began to play, she found herself humming along, *smiling* even, as she carried boxes of booze to the front of the bar. She'd just tucked away the last bit of bourbon when the door flew open and Taz Pullman strode inside.

He headed straight over and settled onto the stool directly in front of Millie.

"What can I get you, cowboy?" Millie asked with a chuckle.

"A small coke would be good."

Millie grabbed a frosted mug and filled it to the brim. She set it down in front of him and rested the palms of her hands on the edge of the bar. "What are you doing in town?"

"Needed some supplies from the feed store. Those damn goats eat more than a herd of cattle."

"The kids?"

"Mom took the twins to Bozeman, but she should be back at my place by now. I ordered ribs and wings to take home."

"I saw George getting busy back there." Millie leaned against the bar. "What's in Bozeman?"

"Santa?" Taz laughed. "I think?"

"It's that time of year," she replied lightly.

"It is." Taz sat back. "What are you doing for Thanksgiving?"

"I'm not sure yet."

The plain truth was, Millie had more invitations for turkey dinner than she knew what to do with. Most folks were aware she had no family close by, a mother in California who she hadn't seen since she was a teenager, along with a smattering of cousins spread across the country, and ever since her father had passed, they made it their mission to make sure she wasn't alone on Thanksgiving and Christmas. Usually, she ended up at Mike Paul's place.

"You doing turkey?" she asked.

"That's the plan. Why don't you come out to the ranch? I know Mom would love to see you." He winked. "She's convinced we're destined to be together."

Millie Sue laughed at that. "She wants to see you settled. You're a thirty-two-year-old bachelor looking after two young kids. I get it."

"Yeah," he murmured, sitting back. "There's that."

George walked out with two large bags and set them on the bar. With a salute, he returned to the kitchen.

"He's a strange guy," Taz said, watching the cook weave through the tables.

"But his ribs are to die for."

"True." Taz paid for his food and drink, then paused before scooping up his dinner. "You see Bridgestone lately?"

"Not in a couple of days. Why?" Millie's gaze dropped, and she grabbed a rag.

"Just wondering how close to the fire you got." He stepped away. "Let me know about Thursday."

Taz left, and with a glance at her watch, Millie realized she needed to get through the bar prep in order to leave early. She grabbed a bunch of lemons and limes and got busy sectioning them. By the time she finished dicing them into small slices, she'd not only cut her finger, which stung like hell, but she managed to get lemon juice in her eye—which, coincidentally, stung worse. She went to the washroom and took five minutes to flush her eye and clean her hands.

Once she was done with that, she loosened her hair from its knot and ran her fingers though the tangles. She'd taken the time to put on makeup this morning and was pleased to see her eyes still popped, though the darn right one was now red. Still, her color was good, and her lips still glistened. She had a change of clothes in her office and made quick work of it, pulling on a faded pair of jeans that fit like a glove, along with a fitted silk blouse the color of denim. She switched out her sneakers for a pair of leather boots that added four inches to her frame, and then threaded a delicate belt through the loops in her jeans, a soft black to match.

Jennifer had arrived for her shift and was behind the bar, and sitting on a bar stool chatting her up like a pro was Mike Paul. They both turned as she approached, with

Mike Paul letting out a long, slow whistle when he spied her.

"Cut it out," she said, setting her butt on the stool beside him.

"What?" he replied with a chuckle. "I can't let you know how good you look?"

"Not with a whistle. What am I, a dog?"

"You're far from that, sister." Jennifer's right eyebrow was raised, hilariously so, and she cocked her head to the side. "I haven't seen you look like this in"—she raised her shoulders—"forever. What's the occasion?"

"I think table four needs your attention," Millie replied dryly, successfully evading an answer.

"Uh-huh." Jennifer grabbed a couple of menus and stepped back. "We're gonna talk at some point, because I need to hear all the details."

"She's right," Mike Paul said softly. "You look really good, Mills."

"You don't look so bad yourself."

"We could do this all night, you know. Trade one compliment for another. But I'm more interested in why you look so damn good. Or at least you confirming my thoughts on the matter."

"And what would those be?"

"Sex." Leave it to Mike Paul to get straight to the point. "You've had lots of sex lately."

Millie Sue considered her answer, but in the end, she couldn't deny the simple truth. She *was* made different by the events of Saturday night. Hell, she'd been walking on clouds ever since. Last night alone, she and Cal had exchanged so many flirty text messages, she'd gotten hot and bothered and pulled out her vibrator. She blushed at the thought.

"There you go with the pink cheeks." Mike Paul sipped from his mug. "Are we talking about a one-time thing? Or was it more of a sex Olympics kind of deal?"

"What do you think?"

His gaze fell to her neck where she knew love bites hid underneath a layer of makeup. But he had laser eyes, and they widened. "Olympics, for sure."

She was quiet for a few moments and then spoke quietly. "I didn't plan for it to happen."

"I know."

"He's like my kryptonite."

"For what it's worth, I think you're his as well."

"I'm seeing him again tonight. He's picking me up here."

"Hell, Mills, I knew you didn't clean up like that for me." Mike Paul chuckled.

"Am I crazy to be doing this?"

Mike Paul sighed and then leaned his elbows on the bar. He played with the rim of his mug and seemed to be struggling with his words. After a few seconds, he shrugged.

"I don't think you're crazy, Millie. I think you're human. I think you can't control who you give your heart to. Not even if you try. That connection is always there. In fact, I think the harder a person tries to sever it, the stronger it gets." He looked at her, and she saw his concern. "And I don't doubt that Cal feels the same. It was always like that with you two."

"I feel like there's a 'but' in there."

"Promise me you'll be careful. That you won't get carried away in the moment and in the passion, because we all know how this song ends, don't we?"

Millie nodded slowly and clasped her friend's hands between hers. "For such a player, you seem to know a lot about human nature. Don't worry about me. I know how the song ends because I wrote it. I would say that I'd guard my heart, but we both know that's a lost cause. The new scars will heal. They did the last time."

She didn't want to think of those dark days. Not now.

"I feel alive again. I've been going through the motions of living for so long, I forgot what it feels like to let go." She was surprised at how deep their conversation had gotten. "To really live and be vulnerable. To give and take. I don't look at that as a negative or being foolish, even if it bites me in the ass."

"It probably will," Mike Paul said softly.

"Yes, but right now I choose to look at that as a gift."

"You're something else, you know that?" Mike Paul leaned closer and whispered, "He knows it, Mills. He always has."

"What are you two up to?"

Startled, Millie nearly fell off her stool and turned, heart pounding at the sound of his voice. Cal stood a few inches from them. His hair shone under the lights, the waves curling around the thick black cable-knit sweater he wore. His black leather jacket was unzipped, his jeans faded and worn. He hadn't shaved, but the shadow only enhanced his strong jaw.

He was literally the hottest man on the planet, and her body reacted on sight. It was visceral and heated and so damn strong.

As soon as she met his gaze, her heart fluttered, her stomach twisted, and she had to stick her hands in the back pockets of her jeans because they were shaking.

What. The. Hell.

She was a junkie. A full-blown Cal Bridgestone junkie.

"Eyes off the prize, sport." Mike Paul grinned and got to his feet. He clapped Cal on the back. "You gonna stay for a drink?"

"No." His answer was swift, his attention focused solely on Millie Sue. "We're leaving." Ignoring their friend, Cal slid his arms around Millie and pulled her close. His nose grazed the side of her neck, followed by his lips, and before she had a chance to form a sentence or say a word, his mouth closed over hers.

Cal Bridgestone kissed Millie Sue so thoroughly that her knees buckled. If not for his arms around her, she would have ended up on the floor, a heavy dose of Cal Bridgestone lust to thank for it. His hands were in her hair, down her butt, and his mouth was relentless. His kiss was both tender and strong, and when they finally came up for air, she could barely breathe.

"I missed you," Cal said softly, his voice low and intimate.

"I'd say get a room, but clearly, you don't care."

They ignored Mike Paul. Heck, there could have been one hundred people in the Sundowner and Millie Sue couldn't see them. All she saw was the man in front of her.

She probably should have thought about the conversation she'd just had. The one where she declared her intent to be careful. To guard her heart. Because if she had, she might have pulled away, put some distance between her and Cal and taken things slowly. But the molten heat between them took over, and all thoughts of caution left as quick as they'd come.

She could only think about the promise of later. When they were alone in her bed with all that time and energy to spend on each other. When he'd tell stories that made her laugh and kiss her until she couldn't think straight. And she would use her body to show him what her words couldn't say.

The thing was, for a woman who was used to being left

behind, later wasn't generally something she liked to think about. But as she slipped her hand into Cal's big one, and he led them out of the Sundowner, she decided that for now, later would be okay.

It was the *much* later she would have problems with.

CHAPTER 18

Wednesday was hopping mad in Big Bend. With the holidays looming and all stores and businesses closed for Thursday, last-minute shopping seemed to be on the minds of a lot of folks. Christmas decorations were up in the downtown square, a large tree lit to the nines, full of twinkling lights in a myriad of colors. It was a welcome sight to those who wandered through the core with hot chocolate and dogs and kids, most of whom were strangers to Big Bend—families staying in the chalets near the ski hills about twenty minutes away.

While the locals were running errands and doing last-minute food shopping, the tourists fed the tills of boutiques and the shops that lined the city center. Cal saw Mrs. Winger outside her bakery, Sugar Kiss, chatting animatedly with a family. He smiled when he spied the treats in her window, a new idea in his head.

He found parking a few hundred feet away and exited the truck, then made his way up the street.

Mrs. Winger looked pretty much the same, except her hair was whiter, her hips a tad wider, and her smile just as big. She spied him at about the same time the family did. A young girl, maybe fifteen or so, started to jump up and down, phone out and voice high.

"Oh my God, oh my God, oh my God," she squealed.

Cal politely posed for a few selfies, signed a napkin provided by Mrs. Winger, which made the teenager nearly faint, and then he followed the older lady into Sugar Kiss. The woman locked up and turned the sign from *Open* to *Closed*.

"Calvin Bridgestone. What a nice surprise," Mrs. Winger said as she ambled behind the counter. "You're in luck," she winked. "I'm done for the day and heading home to my grandbabies, but I can get you some treats before I do." She grabbed a paper bag. "You remember my Ginny?"

Big smile. Big personality. Smart and funny. "I sure do," Cal replied. "She damn near kicked my butt from here to California senior year."

"Oh?" Mrs. Winger raised an eyebrow. "I don't doubt you deserved it."

"A prank gone wrong," was all he was going to say.

"Well, she married Walter Davidson straight out of high school, and they have five kids."

"You don't say."

"They keep us busy, that's for sure. Especially the oldest, Janey. She's a firecracker, that one."

"Just like her mama, then."

Mrs. Winger chuckled. "That's for sure. Now, what can I get you?"

"An assortment would be great."

As the woman got busy filling up the bag with a variety of sweets and pastries, she kept up the conversation.

"How's your daddy? I hear he's off the booze."

"Apparently." His reply was forced. Manley Bridgestone wasn't his idea of a topic of conversation.

"It's hard, breaking that kind of behavior, but he looked mighty fine to me the last time he was I town."

Cal nodded but remained silent.

"I hear Bent's home for the holidays. We were all so concerned about him."

"Picking him up when I leave here."

"That's wonderful." She eyed him over the top of the display case. "He still keeping company with that woman?"

Cal didn't have to hear a name to know who she was talking about. "I don't know," he replied truthfully. That was a conversation he hadn't yet had with his brother.

"Tell you what I do know." Mrs. Winger made a noise and shook her head. "I hear you been keeping company with our Millie Sue."

Startled at her direct way, he fumbled over an answer. "Well, we've always... I mean, I ran into her when I got back to town and uh......" he finished lamely.

"Did you now." The older woman's mouth was pursed tight, though her eyes were kind. "She's had a rough go of it, with her daddy passing and the rest of it."

Shame had Cal averting his gaze. Again, a conversation he hadn't had with Millie. He'd made it back for the funeral, though no one knew but Ivy. For reasons he didn't quite understand even now, he'd kept to himself and hidden at the back of the church, leaving before he'd been spotted.

"I was sad to hear about Dave." And he was. For a time, the man had been like a father to Cal.

Mrs. Winger bagged up the order and walked to the till, where she handed it to Cal. "That girl is special."

Again, the directness of her gaze was concerting. "She is."

The two of them held eye contact for a few seconds, and

then Mrs. Winger exhaled. "Well, you just make sure you treat her right this time around, Calvin, or I might have to get Ginny to ride on out to that ranch of yours and kick your butt to California."

Before he had time to reply to that, she shooed him away. "I don't want money—"

"But Mrs. Winger." He reached into his pocket for cash.

"No buts. They're on the house. Now go on and get your brother home to his baby. Nothing makes a person heal inside and out more than being home with family. I wish you a happy Thanksgiving. Please give my best to Bent."

With that, he was ushered out of Sugar Kiss.

The early snow was still around, and his feet crunched over it as he jogged back to his truck. He waved at folks he knew, though no one else stopped him for a photo. Not surprising since folks around these parts didn't seem to share the same opinion as the teenager from before. He was still a part of them. Still just a guy from Big Bend.

By the time he parked at the entrance to the hospital and made it up to the third floor, it was past four. He spied Mackenzie at the nurse's station, head buried in her tablet.

"Hey," he said, walking up to her.

"Hey yourself." Her ponytail was coming undone, long wisps of hair around her neck, and there was a smattering of what looked like coffee stains on the front of her white jacket. Her expressive eyes seemed dull somehow, and he thought she looked tired.

"Everything okay?"

"Yes, it will be." Her voice was strained.

"What's going on? Anything I can do?"

She blew out a long breath. "Nope. It's just some days, the things I see. The things people do to other people is unforgiving. Normally, I have a box I put that stuff into and tuck it away for another time to process, but today, I can't seem to do that. Not when there're kids involved."

"I'm sorry."

"I am too." Mackenzie motioned toward Bent's room. "Don't worry about me. I'm leaving here in an hour, and I'll be fine. But your brother is ready to go, and he's chomping at the bit to get out of here. I've emailed you his care program, and a nurse will be stopping in every day to get his vitals, look at the incision on his scalp, and keep it clean, among other things. Don't forget the bag of meds on the table in his room. I've also arranged for the pharmacy to auto-replenish as needed. You'll have to bring him to your family doctor in two weeks for a checkup, but he's doing great."

"Thanks, Mack." He couldn't keep the smile off his face if he tried.

"I'm glad you're sticking around, Cal. Always nice when one of ours comes home."

He walked into his brother's room to find three nurses fussing over him. Dressed in a warm tracksuit, Benton was in a wheelchair, his right leg in a cast. His head, which had been shaved for surgery, was bare, and though he'd lost weight from his hospital stay, he looked better than he had only days earlier, despite black eyes and bruising along his right cheek.

"Benton," Cal said, striding over to him. "Time to get you home, brother."

"Do you mind?" The nurse closest to Cal produced a cell phone, and he stepped away from Bent, allowing all three nurses to crowd around him for a photo. Once that was done, he grabbed a large blanket from the bed and set it on Bent's lap, then rolled him out into the hall.

"Goodbye, Benton," Jane Lawson said as they sailed past.

She was behind the nurse's desk and got to her feet to wave. It was echoed by everyone they saw on their way down. Cal wrapped the blanket around his brother and pushed him to within a foot of the truck.

"Damn, Cal. Nothing says asshole like spending an entire year's wages on a truck."

He helped Bent onto the passenger seat and buckled him in.

"I know that. But wait until you see how she rides."

The trip out to the ranch seemed to take less time than it should have. Cal had a favorite music station playing softly, and the two men made small talk about pretty much everything other than the things they should have been talking about. Scarlett. Manley. *Millie Sue.*

Cal told Bent that they had a Christmas tree ready to go.

Bent asked after the cattle.

Cal then offered up some advice on a few horses coming up for auction he felt would be a great addition to the Triple B's breeding program.

Then Bent asked after Cal's tour, mainly the canceled dates situation.

Their conversation went like that until they pulled up to the house. Cal barely got the truck into Park before the front door flew open and Nora came running down the steps. Dressed in pink from head to toe, she sported a shiny turtleneck two sizes too small, a tutu that was adorned with enough bling to make a rapper take notice, and silver tights tucked into her favorite blue cowboy boots. One of her pigtails hung low, the tie nearly out, while the other stood at attention like a soldier.

"Daddy!" she squealed, jumping up and down impatiently while Cal grabbed the crutches he'd stowed earlier and helped Benton out of the truck. "You're all better, except your face still looks yucky."

"Hey. Princess," Bent said softly, wincing as his daughter wrapped her arms around his midsection.

"Your dad's ribs are sore. Remember what we talked about?" Cal said gently.

Nora's arms fell away from her father, and, all serious, she turned to her uncle. "Yes. I know, but sometimes I forget when I get full up with happiness. It's so big, I have to let it out." She scrunched up her face "Sorry, Daddy."

"I'm not complaining, sweets. I'll take your hugs all day long."

"Come inside and I can give you one too."

Both men turned as Millie Sue appeared on the porch. She was dressed simply in jeans and a T-shirt, with the biggest, fuzziest pink slippers Cal had ever seen. Her hair was loose, just the way he liked, and fell in soft waves around her shoulders.

"Come on, Nora, let Cal help your father up the stairs."

The little girl bounded up the steps and disappeared. The sound of Millie's voice was all it took to stoke the fire in his gut, and Cal swallowed thickly, unable to take his eyes off her.

"I'll see you both inside." And then she was gone.

Benton looked to Cal, who cleared his throat. "I asked Millie Sue to pick up Nora from school."

"Clearly, we've got lots to talk about." Bent winced a bit as he tried to keep his weight off his broken leg. "And Ry?"

Cal slid his arm underneath his brother's, and they slowly made their way to the front door. "He went to the Founder's Cabin." They were on the stoop. "He's bringing Manley for dinner tomorrow."

Benton grunted and shifted his weight a bit. "How do you feel about that?"

Cal wasn't the type to bullshit or lie. "I'm not sure. I've been holding on to a lot of shit for years now, most of it bad, but seeing him the other day was a surprise. He wasn't what I expected."

"He gave up the booze. He's trying, and that's something, isn't it?"

"I guess."

He got Benton through the front door and relaxed. Cal owned three houses, one in Nashville, an apartment in New York City, and the ranch out in California. All of them were expertly decorated by an interior designer who charged more per hour than some folks made in a week. They were big expensive things, equipped with the latest technology, appliances, and furniture so fancy, he didn't use any of it. None of them had ever made him feel like this.

The house was warm and smelled like Christmas. He got Benton settled in a comfortable chair in the living room and slowly exhaled, eyes on the big tree waiting to be decorated, the tray of food and drink on the coffee table, and the little girl waiting anxiously for them to start. He looked at Millie, who watched silently from the shadows, and something inside him shifted. He felt unsure, like a kid learning to walk, and was hot. He doffed his jacket, throat tight and full of words he knew he wouldn't be able to get out.

"I got the turkey ready to go for tomorrow," Millie said, moving closer. "I'm so glad you're home, Bent." She leaned down and kissed his brother on the cheek, then turned to Cal, and whispered, "I should go."

Her eyes shone, her skin was flushed, and that subtle scent, all hers, filled his nostrils.

"Stay," he said simply.

At that moment, it was as if they were the only two on the planet. Millie Sue filled his eyes, his mind, and his soul.

I can't let her go.

"I don't know if I should."

"Stay," he repeated.

She chewed on her bottom lip. "Okay," she said after a few seconds.

He held out his hand, and she took it. Thanksgiving had officially begun, and for the first time in ages, Cal Bridgestone had a lot to be thankful for.

CHAPTER 19

It was early, barely five in the morning, but Millie Sue stared up at the ceiling. There was a sprinkling of glow-in-the-dark stars there, and she remembered lying in this bed so many years ago, counting them. She'd woken a few minutes earlier, and now, as her eyes adjusted to the gloom, she turned onto her side, cheek resting on her palm, watching Cal sleep.

Creepy? Maybe. But she couldn't seem to help herself.

He was beautiful. Heartbreakingly so, and looked much younger at rest. So much like the boy she'd fallen in love with. His hair was messy from their lovemaking, though his face was relaxed, and, it seemed, sporting a bit of a smile. Was he dreaming? Was she a part of it? She reached for him and moved a curl from his forehead, content to drink him in. To savor this moment.

They'd spent the night eating sweets from Mrs. Winger's bakery, decorating the tree, and trading lighthearted stories with Scarlett and Benton. It was nice to see Scarlett smiling and Nora chattering excitedly. But it was the ease between Bent and Cal that made her heart sing. They belonged together, these Bridgestones. When they were united, they were unstoppable. She knew things weren't perfect—the mere mention of Manley was enough to make Cal clam up—but she believed the cracks were receding. She hoped that Cal wouldn't be a stranger to them in the future. That he'd find a way to be a part of their lives, even if his took him from the ranch.

Cal had arranged for Bent's bed to be brought into the office until his leg healed and he could get up the stairs on his own, and by nine o'clock, the man was exhausted. Scarlett took Nora to bed and hadn't come back down, while Cal and Millie got Benton settled in the office.

After that, it hadn't taken long for the two of them to get naked and busy in Cal's old bedroom, which, thankfully, was at the end of the hall on the opposite side of the house from Nora's and Scarlett's.

They didn't talk—not with their mouths, anyway—and by midnight, she was asleep, folded into his arms like she'd been so many times in the past.

God, she'd missed this. Those quiet moments before he was awake.

Don't get too used to it. The whisper was enough to unsettle Millie, and she carefully got out of bed, restless and filled with a need to have some space. Some clarity. She knew she was on the edge of something. Either she'd fall all the way in or be smart about it and stop herself before that happened.

She got dressed and tiptoed downstairs, where she checked on Benton before she headed to the kitchen. She made a pot of coffee and, while it brewed, got the turkey into the oven. Millie was on her second cup when Benton shuffled into the kitchen, crutches in hand.

"You got any more of that?"

Millie got him a cup of coffee. "Do you want some breakfast?"

"I'm not hungry just yet." Benton winced and shifted his weight a bit. "Cal still sleeping?"

"Yes."

"Huh."

She raised an eyebrow, and he cracked a smile. "Are you guys back together?"

"I don't know what we are."

"But you're something."

"We're something." She topped up her cup. "For now."

"You don't think he'll set down roots here again."

"No." She shook her head, that ache from before pressing into her hard. "I think he might try, but it won't work, even though he would like it to."

The two of them sipped their coffee, and the silence was like a comfortable blanket that wrapped around them. But it only lasted for so long.

"I don't know what it is in him, Mills. What that thing is that makes him leave. It's more than his music. More than his fight with our father. It's buried deeper, and that's why it's harder for him to face."

"I'm done trying to figure it out," she said slowly. "I know he'll leave again." She shrugged. "There's no point in overthinking. I have to decide what to do with the time I have. Do I focus on the present and forget about everything else? Take what I can get while I can? I mean, I'm halfway there as it is."

"It'll hurt when he goes."

"It will." She looked at Bent. "It'll hurt if I'm with him or not. Does that make sense?"

"It does."

"God, it's too early for a big deep discussion." Scarlett

strolled into the kitchen with a yawn. "Any more left?" She pointed to the coffee pot. After fixing herself a cup, she slid onto the chair beside Bent.

"Thought pregnant women were supposed to give up coffee," Bent said.

"I can treat myself from to time." Scarlett chuckled. "In moderation." She looked at Millie. "You stayed over."

"It was late and—"

"Please." The woman laughed. "We all know why you stayed over." She glanced down at her belly. "No judging from me on that score."

Millie had heard about the man who'd gotten her pregnant and then deserted her. Scarlett had a tough road ahead, raising a child on her own, and so far hadn't indicated if she was going to her place in New York or staying in Montana.

"Anyone hear from Vivian?" Benton asked.

"Nope." Scarlett made a face. "I sent her a selfie showing off my baby belly, and all she wrote back was some stupid comment about birth control."

That sounded like something Vivian would say, but the boys had always had a soft spot for her.

"Give her a break," Benton said. "She's got stuff she's dealing with too."

"What stuff?" Scarlett demanded, sitting a little straighter. "How do you know what she's got going on?"

"You staying for dinner, Millie?" Bent ignored his sister and concentrated on Millie.

"Of course, she is." Cal joined them, immediately sliding his arm around Millie's shoulders and drawing her in close. He kissed the top of her heard. "Where else would she go?"

Millie frowned and pulled out of Cal's embrace. "What's that supposed to mean?"

His smile faded. "Nothing. I guess I thought you'd be here is all."

Aware that she might be a little hypersensitive, Millie softened her voice. "Thank you for the invite, but I do have plans."

"That so," Cal responded. "I know they're not with Mike Paul because he's coming here later to watch football."

Right. She'd forgotten that.

"I'm going to Taz Pullman's." It was a lie, but it was all she had. She needed to be away from the Bridgestones to get that clarity she so badly needed.

Cal frowned, obviously displeased. "You're going to spend Thanksgiving Day with some rodeo bum rather than here with us?"

"First of all, Taz isn't a rodeo bum. He's a world champion bull rider and he's a good friend. He's got the twins to take care of, and I said I would come."

"Wait a minute," Scarlett interrupted. "Taz Pullman, *the Taz Pullman*, lives in Big Bend?"

"You know who he is?" Cal asked incredulously.

"Everyone knows who he is," Scarlett scoffed, as if her brother was an idiot. "Geez, Cal, you need to look outside your world of music from time to time." She winked at Millie. "God, he's hot."

"He knows it too," Millie quipped.

"Seriously?" Cal's eyes shot daggers at his sister. "Can you come with me?" Cal reached for Millie Sue's hand. Instead of causing a scene no one wanted to see, she let him lead her out of the kitchen into the mudroom, where he closed the door and turned to her.

"You're not going anywhere, Millie Sue. You're staying here."

Millie wasn't sure if it was Cal's tone or her lack of sleep or the emotional crap balled up inside her. But something in her snapped, and she squared her shoulders.

"You think that you actually have some say over what I do and who I do it with?"

"Hell yes, I do. Last night, you were in my bed, not his."

"What does that have to do with it?" she shot back.

Cal looked like he was going to explode. "It has everything to do with it. How can you spend the night with me and then up and leave to go to him?"

"I can do whatever I want. In case you've forgotten, I've been on my own for years. I'm used to calling my own shots. I slept with you, Cal. That's all. It doesn't give you the right to boss me around. I'm not your girlfriend." She took a step back. "I'm just an old lover you're spending time with while you're here, and we both know once Bent's better, you'll be gone."

"You don't know that."

Millie Sue waited a heartbeat as she tried to get her emotions in check. How had they gone from bliss to this mess so fast? Hadn't she just told Benton that she was fine having Cal to herself while he was here, for however long that was? So why was she digging in her heels and forcing a fight?

"I don't want to do this," she said slowly. "I'm not fighting with you."

"I sure as hell do. I thought we were back together. I thought we meant something more."

"Then what? How can we be something more than what we are, which is a part-time fling? We're ex-lovers who still have great sex. That's all."

"You're full of shit."

"Doesn't matter what I am. As soon as Bent is better, you *will* get on that private plane you own, and you *will* fly away.

If we're lucky, we might see you again in the spring. And that's fine. That's the life you chose, but I'm not waiting for you. I'm not going to be that girl. I want..." She brought herself up short before she said too much. Exposed too much.

"What do you want?" He moved closer, but she stepped back, suddenly needing as much distance as she could muster.

"I want more than what you could ever give me." Her words were brutally honest, and Cal's face darkened with anger.

"Don't you think we should talk about this?"

"No." She shook her head vehemently. "I don't. We'll just fight, and I'm not doing that with you. Not again."

"But Mills." Cal ran his hands through all that messy hair. "That's what we do. We fight about stuff and then we make up."

"No, that's what we *did*. Big difference." Millie searched for the right words. "We fought right up until that last night and then we didn't fight anymore." Tears poked her eyes, and she forced them away. She would not cry in front of Cal. "You left before we had a chance to make up. You left before I could..." Her voice cracked, and she reached for the door. "I need to get out of here. We should never have done whatever the hell it is we've been doing." She looked up at him. "I'm done, Cal. I thought I could handle this. Thought I could be with you, no strings and all that, because it felt so damn good. But we're always going to be on the wrong side of each other." She stepped back and reached for a place of calm. "We're idiots to think otherwise."

"I don't think I can give you up." His dark eyes glittered, and his pain was real. She saw that.

"That's the thing, though." She opened the door. "It's not up to you."

"You're really leaving."

"I am."

"And the last few nights. Us being together means nothing to you."

"Oh, Cal, you really don't get it."

I'm leaving because it means everything.

She held his gaze for a heartbeat and then left him in the mudroom. She sailed past the kitchen and grabbed her coat off the rack near the door, along with her purse. One minute later, she was in her cold truck, barreling down the long driveway that would eventually lead to the main road.

When she walked into her home, Mr. Higgins greeted her loudly. Millie looked around her empty place, bereft of any kind of Christmas decoration, of any warmth, really, and swiped at the tears that sprang to her eyes.

But it was no use. There was an ache in her that needed letting out. A sense of loss for something she'd never had. Not really.

Millie Sue sank onto her sofa, cuddled Mr. Higgins on her lap, and cried until there were no more tears.

And then she cried some more.

CHAPTER 20

Thanksgiving was a success at the Triple B. That meant, in part, no disagreements, no harsh words, and nothing physical. Easy enough considering it was the politest gathering Cal had been to in his life—not the norm for the Bridgestones.

Ryland and Manley had shown up just before noon, and after a cool hello, Cal retreated to the kitchen. He was still angry over Millie Sue leaving and wished like hell he was off somewhere on his own, so he could think things through properly. He'd been blindsided and wasn't sure who he was angrier with, Millie for leaving, or himself for letting her.

This thing between them wasn't over. Hell, it was only beginning. How could he make her see that? He wanted to get into his truck and drive over there, but Cal knew that would only push her further away. Besides, he wasn't a hotheaded kid anymore. He was a grown-ass man and should act like one. And that meant taking some time. Coming up with a plan.

Thankfully, with the holiday well under way, there were things to do to keep busy. They made a united effort to get the meal ready, though with the turkey already stuffed and in the oven, it wasn't too hard. Rosie had been kind and had done up most of the food prep the day before, which made things easier still.

Scarlett was of no help, she'd never been much in the kitchen, and with Bent out of commission, most of the work of putting it all together fell to Ryland, Cal, and Manley. It had been a long time since he'd done anything in the kitchen, and he had forgotten how much he liked it. Hell, back in the day, there were times Rosie hadn't been able to come out to the ranch, and he and Bent would feed the whole gang. Save for Manley. If he came home at all, he'd spend his evening on the back porch, drinking until he passed out.

Ryland and Cal talked sports and kept the conversation going, while their father seemed content to take a back seat and listen. He chimed in here and there, but was mostly subdued. Eventually, the conversation came around to music, and Cal was surprised to find out his brother was a fan of rap. He scored some points when he let Ryland know that he'd hung with Eminem once in Vegas.

Little Nora was the spark that kept things alive. Her excited chatter, endless questions about everything from Paw Patrol to her rabbit to the baby in Scarlett's belly, was a welcome distraction to Cal. Maybe for all of the Bridgestones. It was hard not to react to a child who found wonder and joy in practically everything. Even the spider she found crawling up the side of the table wasn't just an ordinary spider on the prowl for food. Heck, it was a magical spider who wove magical power into her web.

Cal did insist on rehoming the creature to the mudroom.

Tabitha showed up just in time to eat, though who the hell invited her was anyone's guess. Benton seemed as surprised as the rest of them. She came through the front doors like a Gucci-wrapped tornado, a swath of expensive perfume in her wake. She made a big show out of kissing Benton as Cal and Ryland stood watching, but their brother looked more embarrassed than anything. In her expensive clothes, hands dripping in jewels, and sporting enough makeup to make a clown jealous, she didn't belong.

Cal had to give it to her, she made an effort, though cracks began to show somewhere between coffee and dessert. Nora reached for her second hot cinnamon bun, baked the day before by Rosie, when Tabitha tapped her wrist and smiled.

"I think that's enough sweets, don't you?"

"I want another one," Nora said, chin raised defiantly.

"Us girls need to watch our waistlines." Tabitha winked, but her cheeks flushed.

"But they're my favorite." Nora's voice quivered. "Rosie made them for me special because she said I was so good all week."

"If she wants another bun, she can have it." Benton frowned, then gave his daughter a soft smile.

She scooped up a second bun, but picked at it until Scarlett grabbed another and helped herself to a piece of pumpkin pie. "Are you going to mention anything about my waistline?"

Tabitha's lips thinned. "I didn't mean anything by it. I just don't think eating all that sugar is good for a girl her age."

"I'm sure you didn't," Scarlett said under her breath as Cal got up and began to clear the table. His father got up too, but he told him to sit and relax. He wasn't in the mood to be trapped in a room on his own with him. When Ryland joined him, however, he didn't object—there was a lot of cleaning up to do, after all, and it was well over an hour later that he finally got the dishwasher loaded, the leftovers wrapped and put away. Ryland had left with plans to spend the evening with friends, and Cal let the quiet wash over him.

His shoulders were tight and his jaw ached from clenching it. He felt as if he'd just gone ten rounds with Iron Mike. At loose ends and feeling grumpy, he frowned and stared out the window.

"What say we turn that thing upside down?" Mike Paul strode into the kitchen with Ivy.

"Huh?" he asked.

Mike Paul pointed to his mouth. "I'd like to see a smile right about now."

"Don't be a dick," he said.

"I'll try not to be," Mike Paul retorted.

"Can I get you anything?"

Mike Paul shook his head.

"Whiskey?"

"Nah, I'm good." Mike Paul turned to Ivy. "You?"

"Too full."

They wandered back to the living room. Scarlett was curled up in one of the big comfy chairs, while Bent had the sofa, Nora glued to his side. Manley was nowhere to be seen.

"Where's Tabitha?" he asked, mostly to be polite.

"She decided to go home," Bent replied.

"I don't like her." That was from Nora.

"Same," Scarlett quipped.

"Hey," Benton said, "manners."

"But Daddy, she's not nice." Nora squared her little shoulders, indignant. "She's only nice when she's talking to you. She makes faces at me."

"I'm sure she doesn't." Bent sighed and ruffled his daughter's hair.

"And she rolls her eyes like Danny at school does. My teacher says that one day, his eyes are going to get stuck at the back of his head." She paused dramatically. "But so far, they always roll back."

"Nora." Bent's voice was firmer.

"She does," the kid said defiantly.

"She's not wrong." Scarlett giggled. "It's like Dolly Sanders all over again."

"Geez," Mike Paul replied. "Whatever happened to her?"

Dolly Sanders was Bent's first serious girlfriend. The youngest daughter of the richest man in the state, she'd set her sights on Benton when she'd noticed him at a rodeo, and he hadn't stood a chance. In his defense, the girl had the kind of looks that drew attention, with long blonde hair, creamy skin, and big blue eyes.

To a young man coming into his own, she looked like an angel he'd want to dabble with. Two weeks in and every single Bridgestone, save for Bent, knew she was the exact opposite. She was spoiled, judgmental, rude, and full of herself, a side she hid from their brother for months, until one day, he'd walked into the barn and found her yelling at Scarlett and one of the ranch hands. She'd wanted to ride Scarlett's horse, but Scarlett had refused. The ranch hand had gotten involved, which had led to the ruckus. He'd sent her packing. Cal smiled at the memory of the angelic looking girl swearing like a trucker as she hopped into her convertible and drove off, a cloud of dust following her the entire way.

Ivy sidled up to him. "I have to go, Mom's expecting me, but can we talk before I do?"

Cal nodded and followed her into the hallway. "Everything okay?"

"I think I should be asking you that."

He didn't need to ask to know where she was headed. "She was here and now she's not. I don't want to talk about it."

Ivy studied him for a few moments. "If you do, call me. Anytime."

"Thanks."

Ivy pulled on her boots and searched through the pile of hats and mittens until she found hers and pulled it on. She straightened, then grabbed her winter coat. "We've had a hitch with rescheduling three of the European dates, including the one at Wembley. To make them work, we need to shuffle some of the domestic dates."

"Okay. I'm good with whatever you can make work."

"The problem is that we have to move two nights from late January to December." She raised her eyebrows. "Like in two weeks."

Cal frowned. "We'd need to rehearse."

"I was thinking of bringing the guys out here, and you could rehearse in the old barn like you used to do back when you were a nobody."

A spark of joy lit him up, and Cal found himself smiling, liking the idea. The guys and the music would be a distraction, and with the way things were with Millie Sue, he damn well needed all the distraction he could get.

"I like it. I'll call them."

"Already done."

Cal gave her a hug. "This is why I need you. You're always one step ahead."

Ivy backed away. "They'll be here Saturday." She pointed toward the living room. "Tell everyone I said good night."

She paused. "This thing with Tabitha and your brother, is it serious?"

"Hell no," Cal said with a chuckle. "He's just biding time until the right one comes along."

"Or Daisy Mae comes home?"

She left him without waiting for an answer. Outside, snow fell, but the flakes were light and not much of it would stick. Restless, he pulled on his coat and boots and headed outside, eyes on the barns. Funny to think he'd only been out to them once since he'd been home.

It was quiet as he made his way through the dimly lit barn. He was hit by all those smells that would always make him feel like home. Hay. Horses. Straw. Earth. By the time he reached the last stall, that ache that always seemed to be in him had hardened into a ball. He stood in front of Hank's stall and waited. It took less than thirty seconds for a horse to appear, and even though he knew Hank had been put down years ago, it didn't lessen the disappointment.

The large black eyes staring back at him were intelligent, and they belonged to a blue roan, by the looks of it. The horse sniffed at him and moved closer, and he undid the latch to let himself inside. It was a beautiful animal.

Cal let the horse get used to his scent and sound, and after many minutes of gentle talk and soft touches, the horse let him get closer. He ran his hands across its back and down its flank, noting the clean lines.

"You're a beauty," he whispered, resting his forehead against the horse's neck. It whinnied and bobbed its head.

"She's a yearling. One of Wild Blue's."

Cal stilled at the sound of his father's voice, coming at him from the shadows.

"This used to be your favorite place. I don't how many

times your mother would call you in for dinner and I'd find you out here with Hank."

"It's quiet out here," he answered, head cocked to the side, hoping his father would take the hint and leave.

"The kind of quiet a man needs every now and then."

Cal turned around and faced his father. He studied him closely. The anger that usually accompanied any thought of Manley Bridgestone wasn't there to keep him company. Instead, he found himself curious. "What made you quit drinking?"

If his father was surprised at the question, it didn't show, though he lowered his gaze and took a few moments to respond.

"It's not a pretty story."

"I didn't think it would be."

When Manley spoke again, his voice was soft but clear. "I'd been on a ten-day bender, staying at some shit hole in Bozeman. It was winter, February third, if I remember correctly, one of the coldest nights on record. I'd been drinking since noon and stumbled back to the motel from the bar, trying to find my way through the booze and the darkest night imaginable. Not a star in the sky." He heaved a sigh. "I fell, like I often did when I was drunk. But this time, I hit my head real good and knocked myself out. I don't know how long I was passed out. Half an hour, maybe? It was long enough for frostbite to take. Long enough for my breathing to slow, for my heart to follow, even with all that booze in my system. I would have died out there, alone in the dark, except your mother saved me."

Unbelievable. "Don't even," Cal ground out. "Don't bring her into your delusions."

"They're not delusions, Calvin." Manley's eyes were almost fevered, his handsome face anguished. "She came to me, so bright and full of light and warmth. She touched my face and kissed my brow. She told me some things. Things I won't repeat because they're between your Ma and me. But some were truths that I needed to hear. She said if I didn't get up, I'd die that night. And if I didn't stop drinking, I'd die before the year was out."

Manley paused and shoved his hands into the front pockets of his jeans. "I told her that I wanted to die. That I'd wanted to die since the day she left. She said I was being selfish and cowardly and that wasn't the man she'd fallen in love with. Of course, she was right. She made me promise to stop drinking, son, and—"

Son. Cal scowled at the word and cut off his father. "Do you remember the last time we saw each other? I'm not talking about last week at the cabin."

Manley's gaze never wavered, and he made no effort to hide the pain from his eyes. And the shame. They shone in the low light as if lit from inside as he ran a hand over the stubble on his chin. "Beating a son with my own hands isn't something I'll forget."

"No," Cal replied, harshly. "I don't suppose you will." That anger was back and filled his belly with a fire he couldn't ignore. "You put me in the hospital because you caught me playing her guitar, the one she gave me before she died. And then you smashed it until it was nothing but pieces of her scattered on the floor." Even now, the pain of that night was enough to take Cal's breath away. Manley seemed to have shrunk at his words.

The horse, nervous as the energy shifted into something dark and dangerous, began to paw and moved away from the men. Cal knew enough to leave the animal in peace. He left the stall and latched the door, then leaned against it, unwilling to leave, but wishing his father would go the hell away.

Silence blanketed them both, stretched so thin, he thought he would crack. When he'd had it, Cal made to walk past his father, but froze when Manley's voice, heavy with what sounded like sorrow, stopped him in his tracks.

"I'm trying, Calvin. Not just for me or your mother, but for this family."

"You might be trying, Dad, but I don't believe it's enough." He started for the barn doors and didn't bother to keep the bitterness from his voice. "I don't think it will ever be enough."

CHAPTER 21

The Sundowner had always been closed on Black Friday. Millie Sue wasn't exactly sure why, when most businesses were open in town, but it was a tradition she'd kept up after her father died, and this year, she'd been more than happy to.

She needed at least one more day to get herself right. She wasn't in the mood to pretend all was good in her world because she was, in fact, miserable. And the more she thought about that, the angrier she got. Not at Cal. Hell, no. Her current state of misery was her own damn fault.

She should have stayed away from him. Kept things neutral. As it was, all that anger and misery made for great song writing. She'd spent Thursday night playing guitar, writing down lyrics, and coming up with so many new songs, she surprised herself. Taylor Swift would be jealous.

By the time Friday rolled around, her brain was fried, her body numb, and the calluses on her fingers bled. She was more than happy to go shopping in Bozeman with Ivy, because she didn't have to pretend with her. She could be silent and follow her around, and Ivy wouldn't bat an eye.

They hit a couple of malls and some boutiques. Ivy bought some Christmas presents for her mother, while Millie Sue bought new clothes she didn't need and a couple of books she probably wouldn't read. Hey, it's what making an effort looked like. After hours of wandering the town, stopping for lattes, and rummaging through a few more stores, they headed back to Big Bend. Along the way, they decided to stop in to the Bunkhouse, which was the only other watering hole for miles. Located about twenty minutes from town, in the small community of Gulch, it was basically a crossroads, featuring a gas station, corner store, feed mill, and the aforementioned Bunkhouse. Half the size of the Sundowner, it was run by a scruffy man by the name of Abraham, an ex-con who, twenty-five years ago, upon release from the state pen in Wyoming, had ended up in Gulch when the truck he'd hitched a ride in blew its motor.

It was a bit of a rough place, visited mostly by cowboys from the neighboring ranches, but the food was good and simple: burgers, steaks, and fried potatoes. The beer was limited, there was no wine to be had, the liquor was cheap, and the service questionable. It was dark and seedy, like every other honkytonk in existence, and, on this particular Friday, full.

Ivy and Millie walked inside, and as luck would have it, Dodge Skelton, a local rancher, and his current girlfriend, a hairdresser from Big Bend, were just vacating one of only four booths. They grabbed it before anyone else could, ordered up some beer and a couple of burgers, and after Millie took a nice long sip, she began to relax. This feeling she had, of being out of sorts, was getting old. She picked at the label on her longneck, lost in thought.

"Are we going to talk about it?" Ivy prompted gently.

Millie smiled, a small, sad sort of thing, and shrugged.

"Cal said you were at the ranch, but didn't stay for dinner."

"I realized that it's not a good idea after all." Millie's throat was tight, as if it had worked hard to keep all those words and thoughts and feelings inside. "Me and Cal."

"I'm sorry to hear that." Ivy spoke softly.

"Yeah. Me too."

The waitress brought over their burgers, and another round of beers, paid for by some of the cowboys sitting at the bar.

"Well, let's forget about Cal," Ivy said, mouth full of food. "It's Friday night."

"It is."

"And we're in this honkytonk that's playing some half-decent music."

"Right again."

"We've got some boys buying us beer."

Leave it to Ivy to lift her spirits. "We might have to level up and start drinking the hard stuff."

Ivy undid the topknot at her crown, and her hair tumbled around her shoulders. She grabbed up her beer and sucked back half of it. "It's been too long since we got crazy. I think tonight might be the night."

"You think?"

"Look around," Ivy said. "There's no one in here who knows us. We could do all sorts of things with zero consequence."

"Like what?"

"I don't know." Ivy chewed on her bottom lip. "Dance on the tables?"

Millie couldn't keep the grin from her face. "There's no one in here that *you* know, but I personally am acquainted with at least three of the guys sitting up at that bar. They work at Old Chill Ranch."

"Including that good-looking one on the end who bought us these beers?"

Millie glanced over. The man was yummy. And tall. And definitely interested. "Nope. That one, I don't know."

"Good." Ivy sat back and grinned. "I have a feeling before the night's over, we'll know him real good." She signaled the waitress. "Can we have a couple of bourbon sours?"

The woman was Abraham's wife, Darlene. She hitched her shoulders and frowned, eyebrows raised hilariously. "What do you think this is, the Ritz? I can bring you a bourbon but it sure ain't gonna be sour."

"On the rocks, then."

With that, the girls dug into their food, and the drinks kept coming. The jukebox spit out the kind of music that would make anyone dance, and as they downed the cheap bourbon and the boys sidled up to them on the dance floor, Millie felt some of that weight she'd been carrying lift.

She danced and laughed and sang and drank, and then she danced some more. By the time last call rolled around, both she and Ivy were in no shape to drive. In fact, neither of them was in the mood to leave, for that matter. Why would they? Ivy had met a new friend, and while Millie wasn't keen on any of the men, she sure enjoyed the freedom of the moment.

She slipped more money into the jukebox and picked out a couple of classics, first up, "Goodbye Earl" by The Chicks. She and Ivy and their new pal Nikki, a girlfriend to one of the cowpokes at the bar, danced like fiends, and by the time the last song ended, they were sweaty and Millie had tears in her eyes.

"I can't remember the last time I laughed so hard," she said, pushing her hair off her neck.

"Probably because it's been ages since you drank cheap bourbon like it was water." Ivy was flushed and weaving on her feet. She'd definitely had more than Millie Sue. Her eyes widened, fixed on something across the room, but Millie paid no mind. She was too busy rifling through the pockets of her jeans, looking for more change for the jukebox.

"What am I going to do with you two?" Millie turned as Mike Paul walked up to them, shaking his head. "You're both crazy, you know that, right? I've never seen anyone dance like that before."

"Sorry we don't move like ballerinas," Ivy said. "Don't be a party pooper."

"I think Abraham would like to go home, girls," Mike Paul said.

Millie whipped around, mouth open to beg Abraham for one last song, but her nose came into contact with a hard chest, and if not for two strong arms, she would have landed on her ass.

"Hey, there." His voice was molten. Hot chocolate over fire.

Cal.

"Hey yourself," Millie said, chin stuck out in defiance. She had to angle her head a bit in order to see him properly. "Who called you?"

"I did, girlie." Abraham had their coats. His long, frizzled gray hair was covered by a thick hat, and he was dressed in his winter gear. Darlene stood to the side, glaring at them, as if they hadn't just dropped a bucket of cash in the joint.

Abraham pointed to the door. "Trust me, you'll be happy for it in the morning." With that, he handed over the coats and waited impatiently for the girls to get into them. Ivy nearly fell on the floor, which gave Millie the giggles. By the time she got on her own coat, her sides ached from laughing.

She leaned back against Cal, uncaring that her butt was nestled against his crotch. In fact, she liked it. "Let's go," Cal said, gently pushing her in front of him. He shook Abraham's hand. "Thanks for looking out for them."

The parking lot was empty, save for several vehicles parked in various spots. Most likely drunks like Millie. She'd have to make the trek back for hers in the morning.

"You got your keys?" Cal asked as he herded Millie toward the truck.

"Wait," she muttered, searching through her jacket. "You're driving me home?"

"I sure am." He took the keys from her. "Mike Paul's got Ivy. Your truck is better off in your driveway than left here overnight."

She stared up at him stupidly, processing his words. Somewhere in her brain, there was a voice shouting at her to leave. To be anywhere but next to Cal. Where was Ivy? She should get a ride home with her. That made sense.

But Millie's feet didn't move. *Shit.* Only two nights ago, she'd told herself she would never let herself be this close to him again. Never give him the opportunity to poke holes in a defense that was already weak.

"Let's go," he said.

Okay. Get yourself home.

Be smart about this.

Don't say anything.

Not anything stupid, anyway.

Or mushy.

Don't let him touch you.

Don't you dare touch him.

Hot, bothered, and fueled by too much bourbon, she took off her jacket as she jogged to catch up to Cam. He unlocked the truck, and she hopped inside, but not before rolling down the window and shouting across the parking lot, "I love you, Ivy."

"I love you more," echoed back.

Her head fell onto the seat, and she glanced at Cam. "I don't think you should drive me home." Her tongue felt fuzzy, and she had to concentrate to make it work.

"How do you suppose you're going to get there?"

"Cab?"

"Not in Gulch, I'm afraid."

"Right." She shook her head, which was the wrong thing to do. "The truck's spinning."

"I imagine it is." He was amused, she could tell, but Millie didn't care about any of that. She was tired and had had too much to drink, and she closed her eyes, deciding sleep was the only option.

She tried to make herself fall asleep, but it was no good. She opened one of her eyes and studied Cal as he drove. His thick hair curled around the collar of his coat, and she fought the urge to run her hands through it.

God, his jawline was delicious. And his mouth? Forget it. She was no further ahead than she'd been *before* he came back to Big Bend. Why couldn't she make this feeling stop?

"You're too good-looking," she said, sitting up a bit.

He flashed a smile. It made her heart skip. "You think so?"

"Oh yeah. Too good-looking for your own good."

"I'm sorry."

"You should be. If you had bad teeth, I might never have noticed you."

"So, it's the teeth?" Cal chuckled.

"Totally." What the hell was wrong with her? What happened to *keep the mouth shut*?

"I thought it might be my sense of humor."

She laughed at that. "You're the least funny person I know."

"That right?" He glanced at her, and the look in his eyes made her stomach flip, which kept time with her heart, which was beating so fast, she was sure he heard it.

"You couldn't tell a joke to save your life."

"That might be true," Cal said, his voice dropping as he pulled into her driveway. He put the truck in Park. "But I can kiss you out of your pants."

Her mouth dropped open, and she made a sound of... disgust? *Nope*. Need? *Probably*. Want? *Damn straight.*

She didn't get a chance to figure out what it was, because Cal's seat belt was undone, and he leaned toward her. She froze as he gently undid her seat belt. His scent filled her nostrils, that earthy, piney, masculine scent that belonged only to him. Her breath caught, and her gaze dropped to his mouth. The one that could, in fact, kiss her out of her pants.

If she let him.

Heat flooded Millie. It scorched a path from her chest to all of her limbs. The throb between her legs pulsed with an intensity that made her groan, and before she could stop herself, she moved forward, slid her hand up the side of his face and her mouth across his.

At first, the kiss was hesitant, as if he were having doubts, but that fire in Millie burned too hot and impatient. She led the way, her tongue sliding into his mouth and attacking him with a passion that left her head spinning.

"Mills," Cal whispered. He kissed her back, moving

closer yet, his hands in her hair, holding her prisoner as he made her world rock and spin and...

She broke away and, chest heaving, stared up at the man she loved with all her heart. It was the booze that gave her the courage. The booze that made her go against every instinct she had.

"Come inside," she said, breathlessly. To hell with the consequences. She didn't want to think about being smart or protecting her heart.

Long moments passed as the two of them stared at each other without saying a word. Then Cal jumped out of the truck, opened her door, and held her hand as he led her up the walk. Her coat was forgotten, but her body was on fire, so there was no need.

Wordlessly, he unlocked the house and, once inside, shed his boots while she clumsily got out of hers. The room was draped in shadow, which lent an air of taboo, and that made her heart ramp up to the point all she heard was thumping. It was a mantra that sang, *I want this man*. Her chest rose and fell rapidly as she turned toward the hall that led to her bedroom.

Cal followed, and once there, she tried to get out of her clothes, but tripped on something. A hiss and meow told her that something was Mr. Higgins. Off balance, with her shirt halfway off, tangled up in her arms, she stubbed her toe and swore, and would have banged her head off the side of her dresser except Cal caught her.

He chuckled, his breath warm against her neck. "Good thing I'm here."

Cal helped her out of her top, then she yanked down her jeans and stepped out of them, leaving only a lacy bra and thong. She had to put her hand on his chest to steady herself and then reached for him, hungry for another kiss.

Which he obliged. Boy, did he ever.

The kiss was toe-curling. Soft and hard and so thorough, the room spun. His hands kept her upright, which was a miracle because her legs were wet noodles. When she finally came up for air, she was in his arms, and he carried her to the bed. Cal pulled back the covers and gently deposited her there, dropping a kiss to her forehead.

He ran his hands through her hair, pillowing it around her head, and then slid his mouth across hers, a gentle swipe that left her trembling. "I have to go, Mills."

She shook her head and grabbed him, deepening the kiss, wanting so much more. He felt like heaven. Like the top of the mountain in heaven, the one filled with unicorns and rainbows and sparkles. *And fire.* She growled against him, trying her best to pull him onto the bed, but he gently pulled away and took a step back. Head spinning, Millie looked up at him in confusion.

"You're drunk, Millie. We can't."

"I want to."

"So do I," he replied, eyes intense. "You have no idea. But not like this. We'll talk tomorrow, okay? Mike Paul is here to take me out to the ranch. I'll leave your truck keys on the table in the kitchen and lock up."

Then he was gone, and for a few seconds, Millie couldn't believe he'd left her there. Alone. On fire. Wanting him so bad, her entire body ached. Restlessly, she turned over and closed her eyes, then groaned because the bed spun. She *was* drunk. After a few seconds, the bed stopped spinning, and she giggled. Cal was right.

He'd hardly had to try, and he'd kissed her out of her pants.

CHAPTER 22

It was noon when a grumpy and hungover Millie Sue stumbled out of her bedroom. Hair all over the place, still wearing only a bra and thong, she headed straight for the coffee machine and leaned against the counter, head bent until the darn machine spewed forth enough strong java to kickstart a person's heart.

Once she took a few sips and the caffeine took hold, she cracked her neck and stared out the windows into a brilliant, sunny day. It was too nice out there. Totally did not fit her mood.

Her mind rolled back as pieces of the night before clicked into place, and she groaned. What the hell had she done? Practically thrown herself at Cal. He must think she was an idiot. Cold. Hot. Cold. Hot. *HOT.* She pushed him away on one hand, while grabbing hold of him with the other.

Mr. Higgins meowed and brushed up against her legs, purring so loud, she had to give him a scratch or two. The cat headbutted her kneecap, and Millie sank to the floor, balancing her coffee mug, while the feline began to knead her lap. She didn't want to think about the night before, so instead, she closed her eyes and willed her body to relax.

By the time her coffee was done, she was cold, and the willing of the body wasn't working anymore. Shivering, she jumped in the shower, hoping the heat would wipe away her guilt and embarrassment—it didn't—and boy, was she in a mood by the time she was dressed. It was nearly two in the afternoon, and she needed to leave in an hour for the bar. With the Sundowner being closed Friday, they'd be busy, and she had a lot to do before the evening rush. She left her hair towel dried, uncaring that it waved wildly down her back. The skin under her eyes looked bruised, so Millie took some extra care and applied concealer, then ran some mascara over her lashes. A bit of blush on her pale cheeks and clear gloss was all she could muster.

She was popping aspirin like it was candy when there was a knock at the door. She barely had a chance to dry swallow when Mike Paul let himself in and shook snow from his boots.

"You're alive," he said, taking off his coat and boots. He walked over and gave her a hug before pouring himself a cup of coffee. "This is terrible," he said, making a face.

"It's nearly two hours old."

He got busy making himself a fresh pot while she contemplated the idea of having food on a stomach that wasn't exactly happy about it. She was still staring into the cupboard when he sat down at her island.

"I gotta talk to you about something."

Cheeks flushed, Millie turned around, mind working on ways to dispel any knowledge of her wanton behavior the night before. What had Cal told him? That she'd begged him for sex?

"Ivy kissed me last night."

Shock, surprise, and *shock* must have registered on her face, because Mike Paul sat back and shook his head. "I know, right?"

Millie had always suspected there was more to the friendly banter between Mike Paul and Ivy than either one of them would ever admit to.

He took a sip, face about as serious as she'd ever seen him. "The weird thing? I liked it."

"Well, that's good, isn't it?"

"Is it?" He shook his head, genuinely puzzled. "She's not my type at all, which is why I'm confused over these feelings I'm having."

"Because she's not a blonde with big boobs?"

Mike Paul made a face. "Millie, come on."

"She's not a brunette with big boobs?"

He scowled. "Cut it out. You know what I mean."

"No," Millie replied. "I don't."

"She's...well, she's..."

"Smart?" Millie raised an eyebrow. "Funny? Attractive?"

Mike Paul shrugged. "She's frustrating as hell because she's always right. Whenever we get takeout, she eats my food first and leaves me with the shit I didn't want. Her favorite ball team is the Mets which is insane, and she insults every woman I've ever dated."

"Dated is a term we might want to use lightly." Millie laughed.

"What the hell is that supposed to mean?" Mike Paul actually looked offended, which was something that gave Millie Sue great joy. Men were dumb sometimes.

"You don't date, is what it means."

"Yes, I do."

"No, my friend, you don't. You've had relations with practically every single woman who's unattached in the area, including a few who are, but that's as far as it goes. You don't wine and dine. You don't make an effort because you don't care enough to."

Mike Paul frowned. "That's what guys do. It's not my fault I haven't met a woman I want more from."

She supposed he was right.

"And I'm always upfront with whoever I'm with. They know the score. I'm not a complete asshole."

"Just a partial one?"

He scowled. "You're one to talk."

"You're going to give me relationship advice?"

"You're so afraid of love, you're going to let it slip through your fingers. Again."

Anger, blazing hot, rifled through her, and Millie Sue took a step toward him. "You, more than anyone, know what love cost me the last time."

"Are you going to hide behind that forever?"

"I'm not hiding," she bit out, head aching so bad, it was going to overtake the ache that clutched at her heart.

"You're sure as hell not living."

She rounded the table and thumped Mike Paul on the chest. "What the hell is that supposed to mean?"

He looked at her, his expression so genuine, it brought tears to her eyes. "It means exactly what I said. You exist. You eat and sleep. You hang out with me and your cat. You have your bar. You play music from time to time, but the real stuff, the stuff you write, the stuff that matters"—he frowned—"no one gets to hear. Your light is dim without Cal, and it's been amazing to see it come back to life while he's been here."

Millie Sue looked away because, dammit, she didn't want to cry. She gathered her thoughts. "What good is that when he's going to leave again? Cal can't commit to me, even if he wants to. I can't exist in his world, and he refuses to be a part of this one."

"Have you asked him about that?"

"Have you talked to Ivy about these so-called feelings you're having?" she shot back.

He opened his mouth to reply, but snapped it shut before a word was uttered. For the longest time, they stared at each other in silence, and then Mike Paul got to his feet.

"I didn't come here to fight. I love you. You know that. I wasn't sure at first. About you and Cal. But I think this time, you could be happy. The kind of happy that doesn't come easy, but the kind of happy that's worth fighting for." He folded her in his arms. "You didn't give Cal a chance before, Millie. You let him leave without telling him the whole story."

"That's not fair," she said hoarsely.

"No," he replied. "It's not. But it's true. He doesn't know about the baby."

She pulled away, her voice heavy with emotion. "He would have stayed."

"Would that have been so wrong?"

Millie Sue smiled through her tears. "Yes," she replied softly. "At the time, I didn't want him to stay because he had to. I wanted him to stay for me. But I was too young and insecure to ask him to. And now..." Her voice trailed away as she realized the truth.

"Now?" Mike Paul prompted.

"I love him too much to ask him to stay. To give up his dreams. To not be out there in this big world spreading his joy and music. His heart and soul." There it was. The arrow through her heart. "He'd grow to resent me for it. *His* light would dim. I can't have that now, can I?"

She exhaled, feeling a little lighter. There was something

to be said about truth. About knowing the end of the story and being okay with it. "I have to get to the Sundowner. We're expecting a busy night."

Mike Paul got to his feet and kissed her forehead. "I'm headed out to Old Chill Ranch to check on a couple of horses, but I'll see you later."

"You bringing Ivy?" she asked lightly.

"Let's not go there. I'm more confused now than I was when she stuck her tongue down my throat."

"Okay, that's a visual I don't need." She chuckled.

Millie grabbed her purse and searched for her coat before realizing it was in the truck where she'd left it the night before, right around the time she was sticking her tongue down Cal's throat.

She followed her friend into the fresh air and sunlight, pushing all thoughts of Cal aside. She had a Saturday to get through. Then she would ponder the revelations that had come to her.

And maybe, if she were smart, deal with a couple of them.

CHAPTER 23

Cal had the band set up in the old barn, just past the bunkhouse. The acoustics were shit and it was cold and drafty. The acoustics couldn't be helped, but he'd had large heaters brought in and they kept the cold at bay. They went over their setlist a few times, and now, more than six hours after they'd started, packed away their instruments.

By then, it was pushing six and Rosie had been good enough to come out and cook up some fried chicken. With salad and fresh buns as sides, the guys—Ollie, Matty, Jason, and Max—chowed down with gusto, joined by Scarlett and Ryland. Bent made an appearance, said a quick hello, and had some food before heading back to his bed. He still tired easily, but even Cal could see his progress.

Ollie, his drummer, walked over to join Cal at the kitchen island. The guy had at least two inches on Cal and had arms the size of small children. Heavily tatted, with a shaved head and big scruffy beard, he was a man who made most folks wary. Cal had met him the first night he'd spent in Nashville, and the two men bonded over their love of music from the Beatles and Elvis and Nirvana to Waylon and Hank. Ollie, a transplant from England, had become one of the best session players around and was much in demand. He'd had no desire to become part of a band and tour, until he met Cal. And that was something he was glad for. Ollie was the glue that held the band together, and Cal considered him more than a bandmate. He was a friend.

"You're not yourself. Too quiet."

"I guess I have some stuff on my mind," Cal admitted.

"Benton?"

"He's part of it."

"A woman?"

He glanced at Ollie. "That obvious?"

"Only two things will make a man clam up, mate, and they're both female. Either your mum or your girl. From the looks of that video that went viral, I'm guessing it's the girl."

Cal had never shared his story with Ollie, or any of the guys. They knew nothing about his life in Big Bend. Nothing about this family and all its frayed threads, or the woman who'd claimed his heart when they were teenagers. A part of him felt sad that he'd kept all of it locked up tight.

"Her name is Millie Sue."

"She's got some talent. More than her fair share, from what I saw."

Cal smiled at that. "Sure does."

"Why is she here?" Ollie looked puzzled. "With that voice and her looks, she could have made it in Nashville. Hell, she still can."

Cal stared out the window into the darkness, his thoughts on another night, not unlike this one. "I wanted to take her with me. It's all I thought about. Getting the hell out of Big Bend, going to Nashville, and making it. It was my mom's dream when she was a young woman. But she met my dad and he got her pregnant, and her dream died. The night she died, I swore to her that I'd do what she couldn't. That I wouldn't let anything get in the way."

"What about this girl, Millie? Was it her dream too?"

"No." Cal blew out a long breath. " Which is crazy and I couldn't understand it. She had so much talent. More in her little pinky than I did in my whole damn body. I mean, man, that girl could make the coldest bastard on the planet cry like a baby without even trying." He smiled at a memory of Ivy's grandfather, old man Wilkens, bawling his eyes out at Sunday church service while Millie sang "Amazing Grace."

"She was incredible." Cal paused. "Is incredible."

"It's not for everyone," Ollie replied. "It's a tough gig."

"It's not that. She's never been afraid of hard work or putting in the effort to get stuff done."

"Then what?"

Cal frowned, his thoughts scattered, and he had to take a few moments to gather them together so they made sense.

"I think it's this place. Big Bend. Montana. I think it's a life that's simple but fulfilling, about knowing all the folks in town by name, and having Mrs. Winger drop off a hot apple crumble because she heard you were feeling poorly. It's about going to church on Sunday in a suit and tie, and eating too much afterward. Fishing in the summer, skinny-dipping in the jumping pond, and sleeping out under the stars."

His throat was so tight, he couldn't push out any more words if he wanted to. The two men stared through the window into the darkness outside, and after a while, Ollie leaned close.

"Sounds like paradise, if you ask me."

Cal could only nod, trying hard to keep his shit together in the way that men do.

"Well," Ollie said, stepping back from the island. "Seems to me like you have a few things to figure out."

"Yeah? What's that, exactly?"

"You're in love with this woman. Figure that shit out before you lose her for good."

Cal would have denied it, but damned if it wasn't the truth. He'd never fallen out of love with Millie Sue Jenkins. So the question was, what was he going to do about it?"

"What's the other thing?" he asked, mind already racing ahead.

Ollie slapped him on the back. "You need to know whether you're living this dream for yourself, or for your mother. If it's for you, then tweak it, fix it so it works with your lady's way of life. If it's for your mother, then let it go. Hanging on to someone else's dream isn't living, it's pretending to live and not knowing it. And I'm sure as shit am gonna guess your mum wouldn't want you wasting your life living hers. Not when the one thing that can make you truly happy is within your grasp."

Cal took a moment and thought about what the man had just said. Ollie wasn't wrong. It was as if all these little pieces of his life were coming together, clicking into place in a way that made sense. It was a lot to process. He glanced at the clock, noting it was nearly seven, and turned to the rest of the band, an idea forming in his mind.

"How about a trip to Big Bend?"

"What's that?" Matty asked.

"A town with a bar and beer and a stage and ladies."

Matty jumped to his feet and slicked back his shoulder-length hair. A handsome guy sporting a handlebar mustache, he was the group's premiere ladies' man, and no doubt happy to find a new one in Montana. "What are we waiting for? Let's go."

"You might want to grab a couple of guitars."

Matty grinned. "Is this a paying gig, boss?"

"Unsure," Cal replied. "I'll have to see how the night turns out."

"Hey," Scarlett said, jumping to her feet. "If what I think might happen happens, I want to be there."

"What about Bent and Nora?" Cal asked.

"All good," Ryland said. "I'm here. I got him."

With that, Cal and the boys gathered up their gear, loaded the truck, and sped off into the night. The guys were itching to play in front of a crowd, while Cal was happy to play for one person only.

And if he was lucky, she'd get the message.

CHAPTER 24

MILLIE SUE WAS IN THE OFFICE, AT HER DESK, WHEN IVY walked in.

"Why are you hiding in here?" Ivy demanded, flopping onto the chair directly in front of Millie.

She made a face and tossed a receipt into a file folder. "I'm not. I just have a lot of paperwork to catch up on, and since Jennifer is working an extra shift, we're fine for the moment."

Ivy kicked out her legs and twirled a long piece of hair. "I have something to tell you," she said in a rush. "You're not gonna believe it. I can barely believe it." She sat up straight. "And no judging."

Excitement spiraled through her. Millie had been waiting for this. "You shoved your tongue down Mike Paul's throat."

Shock spread across Ivy's face, her eyebrows raised so high, she looked like a clown. "How do you—" Her mouth hung open for a few seconds, and then she swore. "Of course he told you. He's probably told everyone in town. I bet right now, Pastor Allen thinks I'm a Jezebel."

"I don't think so."

"Why wouldn't he?" Ivy shot back.

"He died three years ago."

"Oh." Ivy sank back onto the chair, her legs dangling over the edge. "Who's the new pastor?"

"Do you really care about that?"

"No. I want to talk about Mike Paul."

Millie Sue jumped to her feet. "Hold on a minute. This calls for some extra-special goodies." She crossed the room and grabbed a box of chocolates off the shelf by the door. The good stuff in the gold wrap. She tore it open and let Ivy pick first—of course she took the caramel—then grabbed a decadent piece of heaven for herself. She shoved it into her mouth and winked. "Now talk to me."

"He took me home the other night."

"Yes. I was there. I know."

"He walked me to my door."

"Don't you mean carried?" Millie joked.

Ignoring the obvious barb, Ivy continued. "We were arguing."

"Not surprised."

"About the Barbie movie."

"Wait." Millie Sue laughed. "He saw that?"

"No," Ivy replied. "And that's the problem. First off, he's a man."

"Right."

"And secondly, he's a man, for God's sake."

"I think I see where you're going with this."

"'Cause thirdly, how can you have an opinion about something like Barbie if you have balls and haven't seen the movie?"

"I guess that's a valid argument." Millie reached for another chocolate. "What was your mountain?"

"Mountain?" Ivy looked confused.

"The thing you wouldn't give up? The argument at the top of your mountain?"

"Oh." She blushed. "I don't really remember on account of me being drunk. I might have tripped, and then he grabbed me by the waist, and then I...well, that's when I shoved my tongue down his throat."

"I see."

"Don't be facetious."

"I'm not," Millie said. "I'm trying to visualize two of my best friends making out."

"It was hot." Ivy jumped to her feet and began to pace. "So hot."

"He's a good kisser."

"What?!" Ivy stopped mid-pace. "You've kissed him?"

Millie Sue shrugged. "We had a moment. Once."

Ivy looked horrified. "You two didn't..."

"No!" Now it was Millie's turn to be horrified. "God, no. We had one kiss and it was awful, and we both agreed that we could only be friends."

"Our kiss was amazing. What does that mean?"

"It means that maybe you should explore it. Didn't you want to do more?"

"Oh, we did," Ivy exclaimed. "We did some exploring on my sofa and then on the kitchen table." Her eyes were big circles. "Twice." She paused, chewing her bottom lip. "He didn't tell you that?"

"No."

"That's kind of shocking, isn't it? I mean, guys share that stuff all the time."

"This feels different to me."

Ivy made a face. "It's Mike Paul. He's the biggest player in the county. Hell, in all of Montana, for that matter. The vet who does house calls, and not just to check on the animals, if you know what I mean. He's not the settling-down type."

"And you are?"

Ivy shrugged, clearly confused. "I didn't think I was. I like my life. All the travel and meeting new people and the craziness of the music business. Cal and I are the same. We don't see Big Bend as home."

Millie kept her expression blank, even as Ivy rushed to apologize for her blunder.

"I didn't mean, I...oh God, that didn't come out right."

"It's okay." Millie got up. "Don't apologize for being honest. Cal and I are complicated. And truthfully, right now, I'm probably more confused than you are."

"Does that mean you're getting back together?"

Millie Sue slowly shrugged. "I know what I want. I don't know if I can have it." She smiled, though it didn't quite reach her eyes. "Not every love story has a happy ending. Sometimes two people are meant for each other, but that doesn't mean they should be together."

"I call bullshit. Sorry, Millie, but don't you think you should at least try? You're both very different people now. You're grown-ass adults with the tools and capability of dealing with problems." She tossed a piece of chocolate into her mouth. "We live in a world that can be hard and cold and unfair. Love is the only thing that makes it all worth it. Come on, Mills, every song you've ever written, every song Cal has ever written, has been about love. If you have a chance at it, why wouldn't you fight to keep it?"

The conversation had turned heavy, and Millie Sue was searching for a joke or something funny to lighten things up when her office door opened, and Mike Paul strode in. If he was surprised to see Ivy, it didn't show.

"You need to come out to the bar."

Irritated, Millie Sue was about to tell Mike Paul where he could stuff it, when he interrupted her.

"Cal's here. He's on stage. And he's waiting."

Cement took hold, and she couldn't move. She hadn't talked to Cal since she'd thrown herself at him the night before. He'd sent two messages asking how she was feeling, but she'd been too embarrassed to reply. Cheeks red and heated, she waited a few moments, but then Ivy pushed her, and the cement crumbled.

She followed her friends out into a hushed bar, where the only sound was the slow strumming of a guitar. The melody wasn't something she'd heard before. It was full of minor notes, the kind that tugged at a heart and enveloped a soul.

She walked to the bar and stood off to the side, eyes on stage as Cal peered back at her. He looked so damn good, dressed in old worn jeans and a simple black T-shirt. His handsome face was framed by five o'clock shadow, and his eyes glittered from the stage lights trained on him.

His band was with him, but they were silent as he strummed the hypnotic melody, and when he began to talk, the entire bar was silent, save for Cal.

"I went to Nashville to make a name for myself. I wanted to make it big." Cheers rang out at his words, and he played on. "I thought it was what I needed to be happy. And I was for a while. My songs went to number one. I was on the road all the time. When I was off, I had the big spread in Tennessee and a ranch out in California." He shrugged. "I've spent exactly three nights at that place. Kind of silly, don't you think?"

He strummed a few more bars and then stopped. "I came home because my brother needed me. Because my family needed me. It was broken, and I was a big part of that. It took time, more time than it should have, for me to know I had to work at mending some fences. I left Big Bend because I thought it was the only way for me to reach for the stars. To have what it was I needed to be happy. But I was an idiot, because what I need to be happy, what I need for my heart and my soul, is right here." He paused and, with the bright lights shining in his eyes, shaded his face with his hand so that he could see her.

"Millie Sue Jenkins." He smiled, and her heart ached at the sight of it. "You been tattooed into my skin since the day we met. There isn't a memory in my mind that doesn't have you in it. I know you think we can't be together. That our worlds are too different. But I'm here right now telling you that they don't have to be. I'm done being afraid to take what I want. Afraid to do whatever it takes to get that. And what that is, is making you happy. Because you make me happy. You make me still, so that I can see. You make me calm, so that I can rest. And you make me mad, so that we can make up."

A loud cheer rang out at that, and Mike Paul kissed the top of her head before pushing her forward, toward the stage.

"I love you, Mills. I'm not leaving again." He winked. "Though I do have to get up on stage on occasion."

"Hell yes," someone shouted.

"But if you're not with me when I'm doing it, then I'm coming right back home to you." He paused, and she saw his heart in his eyes. "That's if you'll have me."

White noise rang in her ears, and Millie Sue felt as if she was in the middle of a storm. She couldn't move. She couldn't talk. She could do nothing but watch as he set down his guitar and hopped off the stage. The crowd fell back, giving him space, and he didn't stop until he was inches from her. So close she could count his eyelashes, feel his heat, smell his aftershave.

"What do you say, Millie?"

The ground gave way, her feet were released, and she jumped into his arms, holding him fast as her mouth devoured his. She kissed him until her head spun and her knees went weak. And then she kissed him some more. When they finally came up for air, Cal looked at the crowd around them and quipped, "I guess that means yes."

He set her down and then held out his hand. "You care to join me on stage?"

Her heart was pounding out of her chest. It had to be. There was no room inside because it was too full. Cal followed her onto the stage, and someone handed her a guitar. Automatically, she tuned it and then turned to Cal, waiting—for what, she had no idea, but that was okay. She wasn't alone.

He began to play the melody he'd been strumming earlier, and she quickly followed suit, waiting for him to sing. When he did, she found herself rooted in place, listening to his warm, rich voice sing a song about a girl with blue eyes and freckles. A girl who'd stolen his heart. One he'd lost and then found again. By the time he got round to the chorus for the second time, she joined in, her harmony so perfect, it made most folks cry.

It was a night spoken of fondly for many months to come. The night one of their own came home for good. And as the last of them cleared out of the Sundowner many hours later, it was a night that had only begun for Millie.

She said goodbye to Ivy and Mike Paul, the last two to leave, and turned to face the only man who made her heart sing. A small smile tugged at her mouth. "What now?"

Cal grabbed hold of her chin and slid his mouth along her jaw until he claimed her mouth in a soft, gentle kiss. Then he nipped at her throat and murmured, "I'm taking you back to your place. It's time to get naked."

With that, he scooped her into his arms, and she laid her head on his chest. She was exactly where she was supposed to be.

And it felt like home.

CHAPTER 25

Cal had never felt so damn free. So full of promise and hope. He'd also never felt so damn horny. He walked through the front door of Millie's house, and before he was able to set her down, she was ripping at his clothes.

She tore at his jacket and jeans, while he helped her out of her shirt and undies. He had her naked in record time, and damned if it wasn't a sight to see. Her hair was long and wild, the auburn tresses cascading across her shoulders like a silken river. Her breasts, pale white with the rosiest nipples he'd ever seen, beckoned, and he backed her up against the wall, one hand holding both of hers prisoner while he licked and suckled and used his tongue to drive her crazy.

"Jesus, Cal, I'm going to explode before you get a chance to get to the good stuff."

"That so?" He grinned down at her and slid his hand between her legs. She was ready for him, but he had other plans. "Spread them," he commanded gruffly, then nipped at her shoulder as she complied. He kept his hand there, his fingers kneading and rubbing the sensitive nub between the folds, while his mouth forged a path from her mouth, down her collarbone and chest, down her stomach, until he sank to his knees and gripped her hips.

"Good Lord," she rasped, her hips thrusting in agitation.

"Sweetheart, the good Lord has nothing to do with this." He pillowed soft kisses across her lower belly, smiling when she swore and tried to offer herself up to him. She was impatient, his little minx.

Cal took his time. He kissed every inch of her except the one spot she needed him to kiss the most. By the time he inhaled her scent and took her into his mouth, she began to jerk and moan, and the thing that kept her standing was his arm on her hip. He fed from her. He licked and sucked and used his tongue the way a devil would, and it didn't take long for Millie to break apart. Her orgasm was loud the way he liked it. It was wet and furious. Her hands sank into his hair, and he smiled, happy to satisfy his lady.

"That felt so good," she said softly. "I thought I might die."

"There's still time," he quipped. Cal grabbed her up into his arms and kissed her as he walked to her bedroom. The cat jabbed at him with a paw, and he shut the door, his only thought to prolong their pleasure as long as he could.

Millie rolled over, offering up her butt like a treat at a banquet, and he positioned himself behind her, cupping her breasts as she leaned back into him.

"I love you, Millie Sue Jenkins," he growled before sinking fully into her softness. "I'm never letting you go."

They found their rhythm, one only their bodies knew, and as he rocked into her, Cal whispered feverish words of love, spoken in a melody for his lady. They came together, and he held her until she stopped shaking, and then he laid her back, unwilling to leave her warmth. He gave her one last kiss.

"Did you die?" he asked.

"Almost," she replied, lazily. "We might have to try again."

"We've got all the time we need."

DAWN WAS BREAKING when he woke up. Millie was asleep on her side, her lips bruised from his, her neck sporting his mark. Her hair was pillowed around her, a tangled mess he'd been more than happy to play with. The curve of her cheek, the way her neck hollowed, the mole beneath her right ear… All these things were burned into memory, and Lord knows he'd thought of them many times over the last few years. But he was here now. With her. And damned if he was letting her go again.

Cal stood back and watched her, wondering if he'd ever felt this kind of peace before. Then his gaze settled on Mr. Higgins, who glared at him from the nightstand beside the bed. The cat had howled at the bedroom door until they'd had no choice but to let him in. Cal had wanted to toss him out into the snow. They'd been friends once, but now…

"We're going to have a problem, you and I." The cat meowed and jumped onto the bed, immediately curling into the pillow Cal had just vacated. He leaned close. "Don't make her choose, pal. I think I got this one in the bag."

He pulled on his boxers and padded into the kitchen. He made a pot of coffee and, after rummaging through the fridge, made a mess of scrambled eggs and cut up some fruit. The eggs he kept covered, to keep in the heat, and he had toast at the ready. Cal crossed into the living room and picked up the old Martin that sat in the corner. He perched on the edge of the sofa and strummed a few chords.

"Still sounds good." He looked up at her soft voice, his heart pounding at the sight of her in his T-shirt and nothing else. She moved toward him and sat at his feet, her chin resting on her knees as she looked up at him. "Do you remember when you gave it to me?"

He nodded. "It was the night I asked you to be my girlfriend."

He played a few more chords and then set down the guitar. He sensed that something was off.

"We're good, right?" he asked, sliding onto the spot beside her. Cal leaned back against the sofa and turned his head so that her eyes were level with his.

"I think so." Her voice was soft. Halting. Concerned, he reached for her.

"Tell me what's bothering you." Her bottom lip quivered, and alarm shot through him.

"I don't think I can tell you. But I can show you. It's something you need to know. I don't want any more secrets. I don't want anything left unsaid between us."

"This sounds serious." He didn't like this sudden turn.

"It is," she replied softly.

Wordlessly, they got up. Showered. Ate.

By the time they were dressed, Cal's mind was working overtime, and his gut was tight with worry. Whatever this was weighed on Millie, but he didn't push her. He took her lead and followed her to the truck. She hopped in, while he went around to the passenger side and buckled up.

The early morning sun spilled diamonds across the fresh snow. In the distance, the mountains rose, their snow-capped peaks sharp and clear against the robin-egg-blue sky. Cal was nervous. He had no idea where they were going.

Or what was on Millie's mind. She was quiet, and he didn't like it, but he knew not to force anything.

They headed toward town, and once there, crossed over Main Street and kept on until they hit a bend and swung around to the Baptist Church. Sunday service wasn't for a couple of hours, but already, there were a few cars parked in the lot. Millie Sue drove to the far end and cut the engine.

She exhaled and offered a small smile, but said nothing.

Cal didn't like the vibe, but kept quiet. Feeling the weight of something coming at him, he remained subdued as he exited the vehicle. He followed Millie as they made their way through the iron gate that led to the cemetery. She stayed on the path that had been carved out by the caretaker and continued along toward the hill on the right, Cal a few steps behind. There, by a big old oak tree, were several gravestones, the tops of them covered by a dusting of snow.

Millie came to a stop, shoved her hands into her coat pockets, and he paused just behind her. A bird chirped from the tree, the small swallow singing to the two of them, a song that sounded more like a lament.

Long moments passed, and when he inched forward, his concern grew when he saw tears on her face. He wiped them, shaking his head. "I don't understand. Why are we here?"

Millie shuddered, her gaze lowered, fixated on one of the tombstones. He turned and frowned, reading the name carved into the granite.

Jaden Lee Jenkins-Bridgestone
An angel come to earth for only a minute.
An angel to look over us for eternity.

. . .

Millie wept as he turned to her, his mind turning back the clock, back to those dark days before he'd left. Could this be...?

"Millie?"

She stared straight ahead, eyes filled with tears, obviously struggling to keep it together. When she spoke, her voice was so low, he had to try real hard to hear her.

"I found out the day you left. That night, I went to the Founder's Cabin to tell you. You were so hyped up about our trip to Nashville, about us going to the city and becoming something more than what we were. I didn't know how to react to that. I only knew that I didn't want to be more. I wanted to be us. To start a new version of us with the miracle growing inside me.

"It's why I told you I couldn't go. And I knew you hated hearing those words. You wanted out of Big Bend so bad. The things we said... Both of us. Awful things. You thought I was hanging on to something that meant nothing, but in reality, I was hanging on to something that meant the absolute world."

"Oh, Mills." Pain sliced him in two, and he took a step forward, but she held up her hand, and he paused, unsure how to proceed. "Why didn't you tell me?"

"I knew that if I did, you would stay. Because you're you. I didn't want you to stay for the baby. I didn't want you to stay because you thought it was the right thing to do. That would have killed the love we had. We would have become broken, bitter people." She swiped at a tear on her face. "I had hope, though. I thought you would come back to me. I thought that you would need me the way I needed you." Her voice was small. "But you didn't come back. You didn't write or call."

"I was screwed up. Hurt that you couldn't see what it meant to me. That you wouldn't at least give it a try. For me."

"I know that now. But back then, I was so young. I only knew that I was scared out of my mind, and I needed to be here. I was going to tell you when the baby came. But..." Her eyes drifted back to the tombstone. "I was nearly eight months along when I noticed he wasn't kicking anymore. At first, I thought, he's just sleeping. He's resting up because the next few weeks are going to be busy, what with being born and all.

"But he never kicked again, and one night, your brother drove me to the hospital. Dad was stuck in Bozeman." She looked at him, so much sorrow in her eyes, it made his heart break. "He was with me with they told me that Jaden had passed. He was there when I delivered him. I didn't hold him. I couldn't, and for that, I will never forgive myself. But Benton did. Benton held him and loved him, and we buried him here."

"I can't believe Bent didn't say a word to me." Bitterness lay beneath his words. And sorrow for a child he'd never known.

"Please don't be mad at Benton. I told him never to tell you. I made him promise. I thought whatever we had died the day you left. And I think a part of me blamed you for our baby's death."

Throat tight, Cal didn't know what to say.

"I was wrong, Cal. So wrong about all of it. And I guess I could blame the fact that I was so young. But the plain truth is that I was a coward. And if you can't forgive me, then I—"

He cut her off right there.

Cal scooped her into his arms and hugged her something fierce. That ball of emotion that had built up inside him exploded, and the two of them swayed together, full of their sorrow and pain for a shared past that wasn't meant to be.

After a good long while, Cal gently let her go. He held her face between his hands and dropped a soft kiss to her trembling mouth.

"I love you," he said. "And I'm here for good." Throat clogged with emotion, he had to work to get the rest out. "I'm so sorry you had to go through this alone." He glanced at the tombstone and felt a kind of sorrow he'd never felt before. A loss of something he'd never known he'd wanted.

"We've wasted so much time." Her voice shook, and she trembled like a leaf.

"That ends today. Right here. With our little boy watching. Keeping us on the straight line." His voice was firm. His conviction strong. He was done running.

"I've loved you since the day I laid eyes on you, Calvin Bridgestone." She slipped her hand into his, and he tucked her up against his side. "But what I feel right now is more. I feel right and good and finally free of this guilt I've been carrying around."

They stayed that way for a good long while, the two of them, silent, taking strength from each other as he grappled with this news, and she gave up her guilt. Eventually, he kissed the top of her head. "Come on," Cal said, drawing her away from the knoll. "What say we head out to the ranch and tell my family the news?"

"And what's that, exactly?"

"That we're getting a license, and I'm putting a ring on that finger of yours just as soon as I can."

"I don't need any of that," she said softly, walking at his side.

"You might not. But I do."

Cal slipped his arm across her shoulder, and the two of them slowly made their way back to the truck. He got in the driver's side and pointed it to the Triple B. The radio was playing, one of his songs, and damned if the woman at his side didn't know every single word.

His heart was full.

It was a good day to be a Bridgestone.

EPILOGUE

Cal found the letters in a square tin box, tucked away on the top shelf behind a pile of crap in the attic. He almost missed it, but sunlight streaming in from the window reflected off it, and, curious, he'd pulled it down.

It took a bit to tug off the lid. He sat down on an old trunk filled with his great-grandmother's clothes and sorted through the box. It was filled with pictures, old snapshots of a very young Manley Bridgestone, and Cal's mother, Joelle. In them, his father was tall and broad-shouldered, though his lanky limbs showed he hadn't quite grown into his frame. His hair was longer than Cal ever remembered it, and in most of the photos, a cigarette dangled from the corner of his mouth. Ryland was the spitting image of him.

But it was his mother who held his attention. As he went through the photos, those of her with her sisters, friends, and most of them with Manley, he saw something he hadn't expected. Something he'd forgotten about. Love.

It was in the way they looked at each other. How Manley's hand rested on her back, or the way she laid her head on his shoulder. There were pictures of them holding hands, with Manley leaning close, whispering into her ear. Some were of them kissing in the middle of a crowd.

They were private moments frozen in time, and Cal felt like a voyeur. He carefully stacked them together and reached for a pile of letters at the bottom of the tin. They were from his mother, addressed to his dad, and he hesitated, thinking that it might cross a line. Who was he to read private correspondence between his parents?

They were tied together in chronological order. He couldn't help himself and gently untied the string. Then sat back and began to read.

May 22, 1984

Dear Manley,

Daddy says I can't come to the rodeo next weekend for Memorial Day.

He says he doesn't want me fooling around with a bunch of no-good cowpokes.

Little does he know I'm getting a ride to Big Bend with Larissa.

I'll meet you by the big red barn.

I love you with all my heart, and I can't wait to be your wife.

Xo

Joelle

March 10, 1985

Dear Manley,

I'm waiting at home for you to come and take me to the hospital.

I'll put this in our special box for you to find.

If I forget to tell you, I want you to know how much I love you.

Our baby is the luckiest child in the whole wide world.

I hope it's a boy, and I hope he's as handsome as you.

I wrote a song about him already.

I'll play it for you when we come home together.

Our family.

Xo

Joelle

SPECIAL BOX? Cal picked up the tin and felt his heart turn over when he spied a piece of masking tape, yellowed with age and curling up on the ends, with the faint markings of a pen that said: Manley's Box. He traced the outline of the letters, put there so long ago by his mother.

And kept reading.

JULY 11, 1993

Dear Manley,

My heart is full. Our little Calvin has arrived, and he looks so much like Benton, it's crazy.

I'm sad you couldn't be here, but I know the ranch has to come first these days.

We're building a life, and I couldn't be happier.

Please give Vivian and Bent a kiss from Mama and tell them they'll see little Calvin tomorrow.

I have a new melody in my head, a song for this special boy.

I can't wait to sing it for you both.

I'll put this in your special box when I get home.

Xo

Joelle

. . .

Cal continued reading for an hour or so, and by the time he reached for the last letter, his throat was clogged with emotion and tears poked the corners of his eyes. It was a lot to process. The love they had. The family they'd built. The good times. Somehow, he'd forgotten about picnics by the jumping pond, hay wagon rides into the twilight, barbecues with the ranch hands, and the dancing. There was always dancing and music. He fingered the last letter that was addressed simply *my love*, and frowned because it was unopened.

He'd come this far. There was no going back. Even so, he hesitated. After a few seconds, he undid the seal and opened it up.

Dear Manley,

If you're reading this, I'm already gone. I know the next few months are going to be rough, and I need to make sure you know some things. Rosie promised she would put this in your box, and I hope you find it sooner rather than later.

That night we met is one I treasure. Me on stage, singing with dreams of making it big, and you watching from stage right, making my heart flutter without even trying. I don't think I realized until this moment that you make me big. Our kids make me big. Know that I'm forever grateful for the love we had. For this home we've built and for the children who fill it. I want you to know I do not regret one single second of our time together. Not even when you forget to put down the toilet seat or leave that godawful glob of toothpaste in my sink. In the future, keep a cloth handy to clean it out.

Promise me you will look after our children with your whole heart, and not with a heart that's broken. They deserve everything. Bent is so serious, he'll hold everything in. You might have to force it out, the pain. And that will be hard, but I need you to be strong. Vivian and Scarlett will need a woman in their life. Rosie is here for them, but after the pain lessens, I hope you find someone else to fill your heart. Please leave room for that.

Calvin, I think, will take this the hardest. He's such a momma's boy and truly owns a piece of me no one else does. It's not that I have favorites, but our spirit is the same. If that makes sense. Please give him that extra bit of love, even on the days you feel black. If he doesn't get it, I fear you might lose him.

And my sweet baby, Ryland. He won't remember me. He won't know how much I loved him. How I sat in the chair by the fire each night as he grew inside me, and I sang to him. Promise me you'll let him know how loved he was. Keep me alive after I've gone. For all my babies.

Remember my love and the song I wrote for you on our wedding night.

All those words are true.

I will be with you. I will love you. Always.

Joelle

P.S. Remember how mad you were when you found your expensive bottle of scotch missing and you blamed your brother for it? It was me. Well, me and Cynthia Henhawk. It was before the church barbecue. The one where I puked into Pastor Allen's lap. I don't regret it. He was a bit of an asshole.

P.P.S. Not Pastor Allen, of course. Your brother.

Cal sat there, staring into the shadows that stuck in the corners of the attic until his vision blurred. After a while, he got to his feet, stiff from sitting for so long. He stretched out his arms and rolled his neck. Then he placed the letters back in the tin box and took it with him.

It was the second week of January. The house was quiet, the kitchen empty. A roast was in the oven, the potatoes already peeled and on the stove ready to boil, along with carrots and green beans. Rosie had prepared things before she'd left for the day. Bent was with Dal looking over some of their horses, and Nora had gone with them. Ryland was in his room doing what seventeen-year-old boys did on a Sunday afternoon, while Scarlett had gone back to New York to pack up her place. She'd be back in a week or so. And Vivian, well, she'd turn up eventually. She usually did.

He turned as Millie walked into the kitchen and smiled. "Where you been?"

"Saying at least twenty Hail Marys to the toilet. I'm surprised you didn't hear me all the way up there."

She was pale, and he pulled her against his chest. "I hate that you feel like this." They'd found out she was pregnant only a week ago.

"It'll pass. Give me a month or two."

"You sure you'll be okay traveling to Australia for the rescheduled shows?"

She snuggled against him. "I'm looking forward to it."

He was over the moon she was joining him on tour, and happier yet that they were coming back to Montana when it was done. He'd already engaged the services of an architect, and when the spring thaw was done, they'd start building their dream home, in a clearing not far from the jumping pond.

Cal breathed her in, this woman he loved, and held for a long time, until she gently disengaged herself from his grasp. "What's going on?"

"I've got something to do."

She watched him, those eyes of hers missing nothing. "Are you okay?"

Cal nodded. "I will be."

She smiled, and his heart turned over. "I'll be here when you get back."

He dropped a kiss onto her mouth, savoring the warmth of her, and then pulled away. He scooped up the tin box on his way out of the house and, shoulders hunched against the cold, got into his truck and pointed it north.

It took longer than normal to get to the road that led to the Founder's Cabin. It was clear of snow, which meant his dad had been out, and he had no issue getting up the hill. He parked and hopped out of the truck, distracted by his thoughts, which was why he didn't see Penny until he heard a sharp bark.

The wolf was coming up the path from the paddock, and just behind her was his father. Bundled up for the cold, Manley wore a sheepskin coat and matching hat. He didn't stop when he spied Cal, but dropped his hand to the scruff on the wolf's neck, assuring the animal all was well. Cal had only seen his father a few times since he'd been back, Christmas being one of them. He'd kept his distance, and, to his father's credit, so had he.

"Come in for a coffee," Manley said, not waiting for an answer.

Cal clutched the tin under his arm and followed him inside. They didn't speak, these two men who circled each other warily. Cal sat down, aware of the wolf watching him from the rug by the fireplace, and accepted a piping cup of java. Black. The way he liked it.

After a while, Manley asked gruffly, "You want some food?"

"I'm good."

"I know you didn't come all this way to talk about the weather. What's this about?" His father looked tired.

"I found this." Cal handed over the tin. Manley took it, and for the longest time, he ran his fingers over the faded markings with his name on it. He sat back and, after a few seconds, gently took off the lid. He stared at the pack of letters as if seeing a ghost.

"I forgot about my box," he said roughly. "Where'd you find this?" His eyes were misted. Haunted.

"In the attic," Cal replied.

His father's fingers trembled as he opened up one letter, read it, and then went on to the next. Cal sat and waited until nearly an hour had passed and there was only one left.

"You read these?" Manley asked.

"Yes." Cal cleared his throat and got to his feet. "The last one was sealed, so I know you never did. I wish you had. Maybe we might not have lost so much time." This was hard, and he had to get it right. "I'm done with holding on to the past. Done with the anger and hurt and blame. She wouldn't want that." His voice caught, and he took a moment. "Read the letter, Dad. Take your time. And when you're done, I'll be waiting outside."

"For what?" Manley's voice shook.

"Sunday dinner with our family."

He left his father, sat in the cab of the truck, and listened to classic country. Cal wasn't sure how long he was out there, but eventually, his father appeared on the porch, dressed in sheepskin once more. He walked over to the truck and opened the door. His eyes were red and swollen, but there was a lightness to him. A calm sort of thing.

"Chicken soup?" Manley asked. "I got some buns here."

"Roast beef." Cal frowned. "You bringing that beast?"

"If you don't mind. Penny doesn't like to be left out. And Nora sure enjoys her."

Cal sat back and put the truck in gear. "No, Dad. I guess I don't mind."

The wolf hopped into the back seat, and Manley buckled himself up front. Cal drove back to the ranch. They didn't talk about the letter. There was no need. They let Cash and Hank fill the gaps of silence between them. And it was enough. Music was the glue that would keep them together.

Cal was finally at peace with his past, and as he drove by the valley where his new home would be built, on this land his family had carved out generations ago, he was content. He would build his life with Millie Sue. They would have a child in the fall.

After so many years of wandering, he was home.

And damned if that didn't make him the happiest man on the planet.

PIECE OF ME

Scarlett Bridgestone doesn't need a man in her life. She's too busy raising a new baby on her own and starting her life over in Montana. But a chance encounter with the dangerously sexy Taz Pullman, sparks something she thought was dead. He's got his own demons, but something about him pulls at her. She knows a dance with this devil might not be the best thing for her.

But the dance just might be worth the risk...

Taz Pullman is a busy man. A former champion bull rider, he's now raising his sister's twins on a ranch in Montana while running his business empire. He misses the life he had—but enjoys the challenge of his situation. What he doesn't need is a woman to complicate things. Especially one with more baggage than the train station. But there's something about Scarlett Bridgestone he can't shake. He knows if they start something up it will get messy.

So why can't he stay away?
Page through for an exclusive sneak peek!

Pre-order your copy today!

The Bridgestones of Montana Book Two

PIECE OF ME

PIECE OF ME SNEAK PEEK!

Scarlett Bridgestone didn't set out to become the number one topic of conversation in Big Bend, it just sort of happened.

On a clear and sunny afternoon, mid-July, she appeared out of nowhere along Main Street, walking at a brisk pace, shoulders square, hair blowing in the wind. Now, normally this isn't a thing that's special or to be talked about, but since Scarlett had come back to Montana in January, no one had seen a lick of her. She'd taken herself off to the Triple B Ranch where all the other Bridgestones lived and all but disappeared.

Some folks thought she'd up and left again what with her having a new baby and all, but others thought she might have had some of that depression young mothers get. Totally understandable on account of no baby-daddy being in the picture. Either way when Mary Margaret Christchurch saw her walk by the old Five and Dime (or more correctly the new Dollar or More) she had to take a second look. And then a third. And then she popped into the Coffee Pot, where she spied some of the women from her hot yoga class.

"I swear to God, Scarlett Bridgestone has gone crazy," she announced with a flourish, her bright orange lips pursed.

"What's that?" Mabel Banks said, eyebrows raised as she poured old Mr. Barclay a fresh coffee.

"Scarlett Bridgestone," Mary Margaret repeated. "She's gone off the deep end." She smoothed an invisible piece of lint from her black yoga pants and waited for a response.

"Ain't that so." Mabel winked at Mr. Barclay, as the elderly man took his coffee, snuck at look at Mary Margaret, and then took a seat by the window to watch the show. He swept off his hat and hunkered down.

Aware that she now had an audience, Mary Margaret set her bag down on the counter and turned to the gathered women. "First off her hair is purple."

"Purple?" One of the ladies said. "You sure about that?"

"I'm as sure as the rain that's coming tomorrow." Mary Margaret shuddered. "And she's got ungodly roots coming through."

"Well, hair color is an individual thing," Mabel chimed in. "Nothing wrong with experimenting."

"It's not just the hair," Mary Margaret continued. "She was wearing a night shirt." A pause for dramatic effect. "A nighty. In public. Have you ever?"

"Oh," the ladies murmured in unison, as if some deadly sin had been committed.

"On her feet? Cowboy boots. Pink ones with fringes."

"My my," Mabel said, palms of her hands on the counter as she leaned forward. "You see how some of these young'uns walk about? Could be a dress is all. I swear my daughter drives her daddy crazy with the getups she wears. Most of her skirts hardly cover her bare ass."

"This was a nighty. With a unicorn on the front." Mary Margaret shook her head. "And she looked so intense, I wouldn't be surprised if she was packing."

"Kind of hard to hide a shot gun in a nighty." Mabel said dryly.

Mary Margaret carried on as if she hadn't heard a thing. She chewed her bottom lip. "She looked *crazy.*" She shrugged. "We all know the apple don't fall too far from the tree so to speak. That family has some history."

Mabel straightened up and frowned. "Did you come in here for anything other than to gossip?"

Mary Margaret scrunched up her face. "Of course, I did." She pointed to the display case. "I'll have a honey crueller and latte to go."

Across town Scarlett, unaware of the spectacle she was creating marched into the post office and paused at the blast of cold air. Her skin was clammy from the heat and her long hair stuck to the neck. She moved it away, and impatiently tapped her toe as she waited for the two ladies in front of her to finish up their business.

God, she was so mad.

The burn in her gut was still there, and uncaring that in fact, she was in an old night shirt, her favorite if anyone wanted to know, she set her shoulders back, and glared at the man behind the counter.

David Wilcox.

He'd been a few years ahead of her in school and had always been a dick. It was as if she had a bullseye tattooed to her body. He used to yank on her braids when they rode the bus home—something he'd do whenever he had the chance. Once day, when she was seven or so, Scarlett had

had enough. She'd jumped over the seat, punched him in the nose, kneed him in the nuts, and bit his cheek.

Scarlett angled her head for a better look. Yup. There it was. Faint but still visible, the scar she'd left behind. She'd gotten into a lot of trouble, but it had been worth it. The boy had never touched her again.

The ladies ahead of her finished up their business and turned around. The one on the left, Jill from the bank, Scarlett knew. The other one looked vaguely familiar, but she wasn't exactly in the mood to sit and think about it.

They slowly walked past her, though they gave a wide berth and didn't say a word. Scarlett watched them out of the corner of her eye until they were gone. The door opened behind her, and if she were paying attention, she would have heard a male voice, but as it was, all of her focus was on one man.

David Wilcox. He was tall, like she remembered, though his midsection had gone soft and hung over his waist, kept in check by a belt pulled too tight. His hair, always thin, was nearly gone save for the round patch that circled his head, and his brown eyes were wide as he looked at her, obviously more than a little concerned.

She smiled to herself. He should be.

Scarlett marched up to the counter and before she had a chance to say anything he spoke.

"Are you okay?"

Lord. Have. Mercy.

"Am I okay?" she said, planting her hands onto the counter. She blew at a wisp of hair that tickled her nose. "No, David, I'm not okay. I'm so far from okay that I had to hop into my brother's truck, which if you've seen it, you'd know how ridiculous it is. I can barely reach the damn gas pedal. And try parking that thing. I couldn't find a spot close by that would fit its big ass, so I had park clear across town by the water tower." She shook her head. "So no, David, I'm not okay."

"Oh, well, I..." He was clearly frustrated.

"Why did you put me on hold this morning and never pick up again?" she interrupted.

His brow furrowed. "This morning?"

"I called about my package?"

"But I—"

"I'm not here to listen to excuses. I want my package. It was supposed to be delivered yesterday, and it didn't come. Then I was told it was to be delivered today, and again nothing." She threw her hands into the air. "You can imagine how pissed off I was when it didn't arrive."

Sweat broke out on David's brow and he nervously, shuffled his feet. "I'm sorry, Scarlett but it—"

"Again," she held up her hand. "I'm not interested in why it didn't come. I'm standing here in my damn nightgown, so you know how serious I am." She thrust out her chin. "I'm not leaving until I have it."

"But Scarlett..." His voice trailed off as she leaned toward him, and he took a step back.

"No buts, David. I will hurt you. Remember the bus?" She made a shooing motion with her hand. "Got get my package."

His gaze moved to just behind her, but at her annoyed tsk, he hopped to attention and disappeared into the back.

"Well, that was entertaining."

Scarlett froze, suddenly aware of an audience. The voice was low, warm, with a hint of rasp and a Texas twang. She didn't recognize it and angled her head to the side, noting a pair of worn brown boots and the frayed edges of jeans that covered long legs. To get a better look she'd have to turn around, and she wasn't in the mood.

"Glad you liked it," she replied lightly, eyes on the door as she waited for Wilcox to bring out her package.

"It's not every day I see a little slip of a woman make a man twice her size crap his pants." A pause. "Makes me wonder."

"Why are you talking to me." Her voice was sharp.

"Just trying to be friendly."

"Well don't be."

"Can't help it. My momma raised me to be a gentleman."

"Good for her." Annoyed, she took a step forward.

"That's not nice," he replied lightly.

"I'm not a nice person."

"I'm beginning to see that," he replied, moving so that he was abreast of her.

Scarlett didn't have to turn her head to know he was tall. Out of the corner of her eye she noted the long, lean lines. The broad shoulders and muscular chest shown to perfection in a plain white T-shirt. She couldn't see his face exactly, but she was guessing it was as interesting as the rest of him.

Not that she was interested.

"Do you think I care what you think of me?"

"I think you're consumed by a package that didn't arrive."

"Well wouldn't you be?" Exasperated she turned to him. Light green eyes stared back at her, fringed by lashes so thick it wasn't fair. His hair was the color of burnt tobacco, the long wavy ends stuck out from beneath a faded old Texas Ranger's ball cap. His features were strong, a square jaw, high cheekbones, and a nose that had been broken more than once. He was wholly masculine, and her mouth went dry as a slow grin touched the corners of a mouth that was meant for sinning.

"I didn't mean to offend you," he said slowly and held out his hand. "I'm—"

"I know who you are," she cut him off.

Taz Pullman.

"That so?"

He was a dangerous man. It took Scarlett all of two seconds to know this. She wanted nothing to do with him.

"I'm sorry to say I'm at a disadvantage. I don't know your name." His smile opened wide. It was ridiculous really. That smile. It was as if the heavens opened up and shone only for him. As if all the birds and unicorns and puppies danced in a circle and sang kumbaya. His charm was off the charts, and she was guessing he knew it.

Screw him, she thought.

She'd tangled with a man like him a year ago. A man who'd nearly broken her. A man who'd left her pregnant and alone and so scared that she'd promised herself it would never happen again.

And yet something about him brought out the devil in her because Scarlett raised an eyebrow and spoke when she damn well should have stayed silent. "You don't need to know my name because we're not friends."

"We could be." There it was. That warmth and charm that made her want to vomit.

"No," she replied. "That's not going to happen."

He was clearly puzzled by her hostility. "Have we met before? Have I done something to you?"

She'd seen him once, last fall when her brother Cal had declared his love for Millie Sue at Sundowner. But back then her light had been dim, hidden beneath the hurt and sadness she'd brought back from Europe. She'd made no effort to interact with anyone. Hell, for the longest time she barely talked to her own family.

It was only after the birth of her son that she'd come alive. Her joy. Her life. Her little Bodhi.

"You don't know me," Scarlett replied, turning back to face the counter as David appeared, face flushed, noticeable pit stains under his arms. In his hands was a package which he gingerly handed over.

"Sorry, it was buried in the back, and I guess Charlie didn't see it."

Suddenly at ease, body loose, Scarlett sank back onto her heels. "Thank you, David," she said sweetly. She grabbed the package and turned around, nearly stumbling when her body betrayed her, and she glanced down at her chest.

"You've got to be kidding me," she muttered from between tight lips. Forget about David's pit stains, they had nothing on the very visible, very round damp circles that suddenly appeared across her chest. Her breasts, tender and hard made her wince and she swore, glancing up as Taz Pullman's gaze lowered.

Great. Just fucking great.

"What are you looking at?" she said, shoving past him.

Head high, shoulders out, Scarlett Bridgestone marched past Taz Pullman, and half the town of Big Bend it seemed. She kept on past the bakery and the bookstore, then crossed the street and walked past the Coffee Pot. She didn't stop until she reached the water tower and Cal's truck, then hopped inside. She tore out of town like a bat out of hell. Her hormones high, the town's gossip mill even higher.

Scarlett Bridgestone knew she'd be the talk of the town for days, maybe weeks and she didn't give a rat's ass. In fact, she giggled as she turned up the radio and barreled down Dry Creek Road.

As she headed back to the ranch, one very curious man glanced at David Wilcox and shook his head.

"Who in hell was that?" Tax Pullman asked, more interested in the answer than he should be. The woman was clearly married. And with a child. But man, she was something else.

Wilcox smiled weakly. "That was Scarlett Bridgestone." He paused dramatically and ran his hand over his bald head. "If you're smart, you'd stay away from her."

Pre order your copy today!

PIECE OF ME

AUTHOR'S NOTE

Hello dear reader!
It's been a while :-)

I am so grateful for you to continue this journey with me, and it feels wonderful to introduce you to a new family, with a host of characters to love with, cry with, and laugh with!

It's been a trying few years for a lot of folks, and like them, I've had a lot of life stuff happening. I had to take a step back and look after me, which while hard, was much needed!

I'm happy to report that writing again is a joy, and I have a LOT of stories left to tell!

As always drop me a line, I do like hearing from readers!

If you loved the book, or even if you didn't, an honest review is always welcome! If you have the time I would love if you could leave one wherever you bought the book! You can also leave a review at Goodreads!

As always, I wish hope you spread love, pay it forward, give someone a hug, and love your family!

Xo
Juliana

ABOUT THE AUTHOR

USA Today bestselling author and 2015 RITA® winner JULIANA STONE fell in love with books in the fifth grade when her teacher introduced her to Tom Sawyer. A tomboy at heart, she splits her time between baseball, books, and music. She's thrilled to be writing young adult as well as adult contemporary romance—books that have garnered starred reviews from *Publishers Weekly* & Booklist—from somewhere in the wilds of Canada.

I love hearing from my readers, and you can find me by clicking the links below! If you want to stay abreast of all happenings, you can sign up for my newsletter

http://www.julianastone.com/contact/

Lastly, if you have the time to leave an honest review of my books at point of purchase, or Goodreads, it would be much appreciated! Every little bit helps!

Xo

Juliana

Please visit me at the my website.

www.julianastone.com

or write to me with this email address

juliana@julianastone.com

All other social media links are below!

ALSO BY JULIANA STONE

The Bridgestones Of Montana

Cover Me Up

PIECE OF ME

The Barker Triplets

Offside

Collide

Conceal

A Barker Family Christmas

Long Road Home

The Family Simon series

Tucker -Free

Jack

Maverick

Teague

Grace

Cooper

The Blackwells of Crystal Lake

You Make Me Weak

You Drive Me Crazy

You Rock My World

You Own My Heart

A Crystal Lake Novel

The Thing About Trouble

That Thing You Do

A Little Bit Of Christmas

Love And Other Things

Love Me Forever

Shake The Frost

Slow Kind Of Love

Standalone Novels

He's All that

The Carousel

Made in the USA
Middletown, DE
21 December 2023